Crannóg 55 autumn 2021

Editorial Board

ISSN 1649-4865
ISBN 978-1-907017-61-2

Cover image: *Rust by Me*, by Bill Hicks
Cover image sourced by Sandra Bunting
Cover design by Wordsonthestreet
Published by Wordsonthestreet for Crannóg magazine   @CrannogM
www.wordsonthestreet.com   @wordsstreet

Comhairle Cathrach na Gaillimhe
Galway City Council

CONTENTS

Submissions for Crannóg 56 open November 1st until November 30th
Publication date is March 25th 2022

Crannóg is published bi-annually in spring and autumn.

Submission Times:
Month of November for spring issue.
Month of May for autumn issue.

We will <u>not read</u> submissions sent outside these times.

POETRY:
Send no more than three poems. Each poem should be under 50 lines.
PROSE:
Send one story. Stories should be under 2,000 words.

We do not accept postal submissions.
When emailing your submission we require three things:
1. *The text of your submission included both in body of email and as a Word attachment (this is to ensure correct layout. We may, however, change your layout to suit our publication).*
2. *A brief bio in the third person. Include this both in body and in attachment.*
3. *A postal address for contributor's copy in the event of publication.*

For full submission details, to learn more about Crannóg Magazine, to purchase copies of the current issue, or take out a subscription, log on to our website:

www.crannogmagazine.com

Síle na gCíoch

Deirdre McGarry

(síle na gcíoch: mediaeval figurative carving of a naked woman displaying an exaggerated vulva often found in churches and on ancient pillars in Ireland)

Hag,
I cling to your power.
Gaping sex, saggy breasts,
rumble tumble womb,
tomb of all dream boys.

No-truck backfoot reel
you blow the breath of thunder,
poke your luck, struggle up.

Dance, jig, squat, fuck,
gobble up the squabble tittle tattle
in your dark cave,
Rattle, grapple, hustle, thump.

All the grubby tricks and deals
drown and suck.

Astonishment

Lisa C. Taylor

I breakfast on the rust of rocks,
whip of wind walker sage,
make art from saffron and taupe,
the sweep of veridian and stone.

Terracotta dawn
reigns over peaks tinselled
with snow.
Bee down and sandbox,
Tawny Crescent and Anise Swallowtail,
the shape of astonishment.

A small mammal crosses
in front of me, followed by another
and another. Plump, brown,
and surprising as rain,
marmot or prairie dog waddle
across a makeshift road
with no edges.

The sun, a balloon, inflates,
suspended in blue.

I am hinged to this place,
its bleeding dusks and arid days,
the way mountains prevail,
barring avalanche or eruption.
Broken pieces reborn as scree
to clamber over,
reaching an owl-coloured plateau,
a feast of tinge and mist.

Nephophobia

Hussain Ahmed

To mourn is a path
towards forgetfulness.

Once, I spent a night
in a room with mama,

she told stories I already knew
of her dead daughter. That night,

a shark attacked me in a dream. But
I woke up to the shrill call to prayer.

A preacher cautioned me about God
and how He may decide me fit

to be housed inside of a fish.

I have not betrayed anyone,
I only confess that I fear the dark sky.

Sue

Helen Daugherty

HE WAS LUCID THAT DAY. She had carried her body from one residential home to another. Harvard House it was called. They would have joked that he was going to Harvard. There were lots of jokes and observations that went unshared now, too many to remember. She'd stack them up in her memory at first, saving them to tell him at some later point, out of habit. The jokes don't work without another person to hear them, though. They might as well have never happened, like the tree not falling in the forest.

The faces that worked there were familiar to her now. It was nice enough, for a place that housed the dying. The room at the end of the Eastern wing was Joe's. The fountain could be heard from his bedroom. Mostly he was sleeping. *Resting*. Expiring was exhausting. It was an ugly thing; it was necessary to medicate your way out of this life, so that others didn't have to look upon your pain, on your realisation, your grief even, as you still lived. So that you transitioned into death in a fog of medicated sleep, crossing over, going into the blackness alone without realising it until it was upon you. Sue had seen it before. A lucidity at the end, even sometimes through the medication, the eyes flashing open, dark and aware suddenly. The cruelty of the hope that that brings, to the relative, to the loved one sitting at the side of the bed, waiting, watching.

Sue froze in the doorway. Today he was up, sitting in a chair, the door to the garden open. Mary was still there, reading to him, propping his head up when it flopped uncomfortably to one side or the other, arranging his pillows. It was unexpected. Sue had to reset herself: she had become accustomed to him being supine and her brain leapt – it wanted to tell her that there had been progress. But it was just the provision of a quality death being carried out here. She felt another hot flush beginning its bloom across her face. Her thoughts weighed against each other. If only she could escape from herself. Underneath her skin there was a war being carried out, fire racing through her veins at any given time and outside she stood in a smoking trainwreck that used to be their lives. She stood uneasily somewhere in between, coming apart, decoupling from herself, detaching, disconnecting, going wrong. One armpit smelled and the other one didn't. She could feel the rash there returning, exacerbated by both using deodorant and not, skin chafing against skin, soul chafing inside body, things coming loose and rattling around. Maybe she could have muddled through it with Joe somehow, but he was gone though he left behind a version of himself for her to wither beside. She mulled over the absence of a scent from her vagina these days standing there in that room. Mary looked at her expectantly.

Sue's face fell into its usual smile. She never knew what to do with herself here. Her arms dangled stupidly at her sides as she shifted her weight to the other foot. Of course, she chatted inanely, as if everything was normal and they were just having a catch-up after work. Her voice bright and warm, skipping over the edges of things. It was bizarre. There was no right way to be, they said. But everything jarred. She itched to be out of there. They could have done this at home. But she was more afraid of that. Even less equipped for that.

Mary left husband and wife alone, a quiet, tactful exit, graciously and piously executed. Sue felt a bubble of hysteria travelling up inside her, a compulsion to run in the opposite direction.

She sat down. Held a dry hand, papery palm sliding across hers and which failed to hold back. She couldn't look at him. Her eyes darted around the outskirts of his face, the pillows, the attachments. His eyes were closed.

She talked about work, about family, and tried to fill the minutes up. He was not there really. There was a window of time in which he swam up out of his fog, responding to her voice, before succumbing to the pain. Before the window of his awareness became too wide, yawning into torture. These glimpses of him were cruel. She didn't want him to go but he was already gone, wasn't he? It's not as if there was any going back from here. May as well go, then. Be out of pain, of need. Of humiliation. He wouldn't have wanted this. But simply stating that in his well days, in his walking around and talking days, didn't change things when they did happen. Unless flights to Switzerland had been booked, your loved ones were instead compelled to watch you slowly die against your wishes. Best seats in the house. His hands moved in hers. She could never have imagined such pain. Her vessel of a bodybrain was not built to contain it. The hope the movement brought was unbearable. *Unfair*. She brought his hand up to her lips and kissed it, puckering her lips against the dry skin.

She was used to the smell. That chemical smell, necrosis of the self. The smell of dying. A tear left her eye, wetting her cheek. She caught it with her tongue, darting it away inside her mouth. She sniffed the tears up her nose, and swallowed them as they travelled down the back of her throat. He started to stir.

'Suzy,' he said.

He was the only one left to call her that. Her parents, her friends from youth. Now she was just good old Sue. Sexless Sue. Mother. Grandmother. Carer. Invisible, menopausal, fat, middle-aged stranger. Still dyeing the hair, for a while.

She couldn't stop the tears. She wasn't supposed to cry. Not here, not now. The nurse had grabbed her hand, squeezed it hard, too hard, insisting that she didn't cry. It'll upset him, she said. He'll give up, she said. Speaking quietly, secretly, through closed teeth, so that only she could hear. That was in the early days after his diagnosis, in the hospital, when there was still hope. Before the best before date had turned into an expiry date. The tears sprang out of her eyes simultaneously and raced each other down her face, one after the other. His hands shook; he was become agitated.

'I'm dying,' he said.

A nurse passed the room, a flash of blue in the corner of her eye. Sue jumped up, extricating herself from the hand that now grasped at hers, rushing to the door.

'He's upset,' she gasped, desperate, wiping her face. She couldn't do this alone. *Help me*. The nurse approached, efficient, calm. Her eyes soft within the professional set of her face. She gently squeezed Sue's arm as she passed her on her way to the patient, crouching down in front of him, looking earnestly into his cringing face.

'Hello, Joe. It's Irene. Is there any pain?' His eyes were still closed but his movements were jerky, his face contorting. It was horrible to watch. Sue was grateful for the presence of the nurse. She would *do* something. Soon Irene was summoning assistance, helping him back into bed, administering more opioids to the canula. Sue stood by the door, fleshy furniture, watching-not watching. Out of the way. It wasn't necessary they said, she didn't want to get in the way she said, you're not in the way they said. His words repeating in her head, trying not to cry, digging her nails into her palms to fill his absence there, to dam the feelings, avoiding the nurses' eyes.

A bad wife, cowardly and weak. She squirmed in a soup of her failure; the fear that had torn her from his side in his moment of need. That would wake her up in the middle of the night and keep her from sleep. She would never speak of it to anyone. He had grasped for her, a drowning man, and she had let him fall, alone. Soon he was settled and she stayed a few minutes more before leaving, scuttling out of Harvard House like a rat, holding her opinion of herself like a poisonous package close to her body.

Stain

Amanda Bell

after Edward Munch's *Puberty*

So here's a thing
beyond control
of will or muscle –

a copper-scented flow
that dries in ridges
while you sleep,

at an unseen
metronome's
relentless bidding.

Now to reconcile
your body to
a contrapuntal rhythm

that quite often
skips a beat:
leaves a trail

of carmine scrawls
– unwitting signatures –
on strangers' sheets.

Per Fumare

Leonore Wilson

The gods were pleased,
weren't they
when that first fragrance man created
was meant to burn –

It was speech to them,
ephemeral whispering,

what I didn't know in early autumn
as I opened the woodstove, and

dropped the fists of poems in
and laid the dry
branches down,
and lit the pyre

and closed the iron doors

and the little windows glowed
gold, the alchemy paused

and seemed
to enter me, and I

watched matter become spirit
and I breathed in the white smoke
escaping into the blue heavens

as a child enters the physical
world, its living soul

crying out with no
thought of place or origin . . .

Love & Covid

Liz McManus

'HELLO, IS THAT SALLY?'

'Well, I'll be damned,' she said, 'Ambrose Marshall.'

'That's me. How are you?'

Outside the kitchen window a cat was stalking a magpie. The bird flew up to rest on the shed roof. In the grass, the cat waited, her tail twitching.

'Where are you calling from?' she asked. She had a memory of the two of them standing in a phone booth on Nassau Street. How long ago was it? Fifty-eight years. Now phone booths were a thing of the past. Ambrose was phoning from Westmeath. Of course, the family farm outside Moate. His voice was louder than she remembered. Probably going deaf. What age was he? Seventy-seven, the same age as she was. Ancient.

'I was just thinking of you when out of the blue, I bumped into a college friend and she gave me your number. Talk about a coincidence.'

She was astonished. 'You were thinking of me?'

In university the girls in her class had been mad about him. 'Ambrose Marshall, or Marshall Ambrose if you prefer,' he had said that day when he sat down beside her in the lecture hall. 'We Prods are fond of surnames.' She and he became friends by accident more than design. They were both studying archaeology and on field trips they paired up. Ambrose wore a cravat inside his frayed shirt and carried a silver cigarette case and spoke in a plummy accent. He was handsome in an old-fashioned squire way but she had found it hard to take him seriously.

Now they were catching up on spouses – he was on his second wife, she was still with Rory. Then the conversation moved on to how they were coping with lockdown.

'I have nightmares that Covid is breaking into this house and wrecking the furniture.'

She laughed. 'And what do you do?'

'Oh, I take out my sword and smite the thing in two. All rather phallic, I suppose.'

She looked at her watch. 'I have to go.'

'May I phone you again?'

'Oh yes, please,' she said, without thinking. 'I'd like that.'

It took her twenty minutes to drive to the day care centre. She liked working with old people and worried that she'd be told to stay home because of Covid. She was only a volunteer and yet the nurse depended on her. It was mainly women who came to the centre: the widows of farm labourers and forestry workers bussed there each morning and, in the evening, brought back to their isolated cottages. Farmers' widows tended towards private nursing homes rather than the health board day care centre. There weren't health boards anymore, Sally reminded herself. Only the HSE. She cut toenails and blowdried hair and chatted to the women and when she went home in the afternoon she wondered why the mundane work lifted her spirits so much. On the day the nurse told her not to come to the centre any more, Sally burst into tears.

'You must understand, dear.' The nurse was gentle. 'At your age you are vulnerable. Anyway I expect the centre will be closed soon, as a precaution.'

'It's only a bit of voluntary work,' she told Ambrose during one of their phone calls. 'I don't know why I got so upset.'

'Covid gets to you in strange ways. I get a buzz from minding my cows. I talk to them a lot.'

She wanted to ask him if he remembered how she had disgraced herself: going to the Trinity Ball with one boy and leaving with another. That night, without a backward glance, she had walked out into the night with Ambrose Marshall. She hadn't had much to drink so she had no excuse except that she was deliriously happy at the sight of him coming towards her through the hot, roaring crowd.

'Will you come upstairs with me?' he had said, lowering his head onto her shoulder. 'To my room?'

The boy she'd come with hadn't even noticed her leaving. He was very drunk and more interested in his mates than he was in her. Even so, she felt guilty for a long time after. Good girls didn't do that kind of thing and she wanted to be good. Until then, her experience of boys had been unsatisfactory: clumsy fumblings in the backs of cars, and heavy petting sessions that had left her cold. Am I frigid? she had fretted.

That night, in the doorway of his rooms in Botany Bay, Ambrose had pulled her close and they had kissed for the first time. It was only after she was married that she understood how much her generation had missed out on: the freedom of the pill, smoking pot, the mad politics, Women's Lib. Compared to her daughter who thought she had it made, all Sally had was a memory of Ambrose Marshall's body on hers, naked, among the rumpled sheets.

Eventually she summoned enough courage to ask him. 'Do you remember that night?'

'Of course I do.'

'When you kissed me that first time,' she said shyly, 'it was the most thrilling kiss I ever had, before or since.'

Silence.

'Are you still there?'

'Do you know,' he said at last, 'that is the nicest thing anyone has ever said to me. I remember everything about that night; you were so excited I could feel your heart beating against my chest. It made me half-crazy. Nothing could have come between us. If we'd been hosed down by a water cannon we wouldn't have noticed.'

She burst out laughing.

'And afterwards, you danced naked for me.'

She shook her head. 'I don't remember that.'

'Well, there you go,' he said, 'I do.'

It was quite innocent, she thought, talking on the phone to an old flame in the middle of a pandemic. All the same she didn't tell her husband. Rory had lost interest in sex a long time ago. So had she, in her own way. After he retired, the garden kept them busy, and the grandchildren, of course. He had his golf and she had her voluntary work. Then the lockdown upended everything. The two of them stuck at home without a route out. She had Ambrose Marshall hidden in her phone but what, she wondered, did her husband have? When the taoiseach announced on television that golf clubs were to be closed, Rory had leapt up, snarling at the screen, *You fucking, fucking bastard.*

'For heaven's sake, Rory,' Sally said. 'Calm down.'

Then she saw the tears in his eyes.

'I am sorry,' she murmured but he had already turned away. Golf was the closest to passion that Rory got these days. If she disappeared in the morning, would he feel as strongly? Covid is hard, she thought, on both of us. That night she moved closer to him in the bed, whispering 'Rory, love ...' but he had already fallen asleep and was snoring.

She looked forward to their aimless conversations.

'That night, how did it happen?' she wondered. 'I mean, I never thought.'

'You must have known that I fancied you,' Ambrose said. 'All those bloody field trips I had to go on just to be with you.'

She was mortified. 'I didn't know.'

As soon as term ended, Ambrose had gone away. Other students got summer jobs picking peas in the south of England or in canning factories. He went to London and wangled himself a job at the British Museum. By the time he returned that September, Sally was already engaged to Rory.

'When this lockdown is over, would you like to meet me?'

Oh yes, she wanted to say but she couldn't.

'How about lunch in my club.'

She smiled. 'You have a club. Why am I not surprised?'

'It's handy when I'm staying in town. It's the only luxury I can afford although to be honest, I can't really afford it.'

'Yes.'

'Yes to lunch?'

They had expected that everything would be back to normal by April but there were delays with the vaccines and a new variant of Covid caused a stir. It was late July before they could even talk about meeting. By then they had both been vaccinated and restrictions had been lifted.

'So we will meet in Dublin,' he said. 'Can't wait.'

It was madness, she thought, but there was no harm in it: two old friends meeting over lunch to reminisce. It wasn't as if she was being unfaithful. Could you be unfaithful to a husband who wasn't bothered? Rory was back out on the golf course, delighted with himself: that was all he wanted.

She looked around the bedroom, at the pictures on the walls, the photos of grandchildren. Here was evidence of the home and family she had made. She was seventy-seven years old, she reminded herself. It made no sense: inside, she was still a girl. She stared at her reflection in the mirror. Would Ambrose even recognise her? She paused for a moment, unable to remember what she was looking for. Ah yes, in the drawer, the black lacy underwear that she hadn't worn for years. Why not? There was no harm in dressing up after months of lockdown and she thought of the elderly women in the day care centre, all gussied up with nowhere to go.

In the front hall of the club, Ambrose was waiting. He took her coat, handed it to the porter and then ushered her into the dimly lit bar where they sat down on high-backed chairs facing each other. Ambrose had weathered well, she thought, with his farmer's tan and his grey hair in need of a cut. His long legs were encased in cavalry twill trousers. For heaven's sake, she wanted to say, who wears cavalry twill nowadays? At the sight of his worn, polished brogues and the leather patches on the elbows of his shabby jacket, she softened.

'You look good enough to eat,' she said.

Smiling, he offered her a menu. 'Now there's a thought.'

The club dining room was like the inside of an auctioneer's showroom, crammed with antique furniture and dust motes in the air. She looked down at the silver cutlery, the cut glass on the table and thought: this could be my last chance. The lacy strap of her bra was digging into her shoulder and she slipped her hand inside the collar of her dress to ease it. When she looked up, Ambrose was watching her with interest. 'Is everything alright?'

She blushed. 'Everything is lovely.'

'Yes,' he said. 'And so are you.'

She knew then what he was going to ask her after lunch was over. This is madness, she wanted to say but the girl inside her resisted. Why not take a risk? She had played safe for too long. Then she remembered that Ambrose had told her about his heart trouble, and the stents the surgeon had put in. How much excitement could he take? She visualised the tabloid headlines, *'OAP Dies in Geriatric Love Nest,'* and she shuddered. The day could end in disaster. What a way to go ... And yet, she thought, there were worse ways. Way to go, as her grandson was fond of saying. Way to go, Granny, heading for a fall.

'Pudding?'

'No, thank you. Just coffee for me, please.'

He leant back in his chair and spread his gnarled fingers on the tablecloth. She gazed down at his wedding ring and then at the gold ring on her own wrinkled hand. Anyone looking at the two of them would think they were an old married couple.

'Will you come upstairs with me,' he said, 'to my room?'

Autumn Leaves: Miles Davis

Byron Beynon

That inner sense of freedom,
a natural balance
with an impulse
to preserve the day,
as the equinox
tilts from a window
with a view of leaves on fire.
The cycle of blues
in a public park,
the elegant air exposed
as fashions parade
with future notes on display.
The fields of funk,
his purity of sound
penetrating early morning streets
heightened by a full October moon,
an instinct for movement
travelling towards
a jazz of universal light.

Empathy

Mark Ward

The craft is adrift in
blackness: a night sea ceilinged with
a starless sky, I coast
in an origami boat.

My toothpick oars were lost
to a fruitless spearing of fish.
An isolation tank
works only with a sure exit.

An echo of the ship
ping forecast shows each comber's height.
I did not realise
you are the entire ocean.

You move and the world fills
with sun. I see my reflection
in the glass. Your bottle
stoppered; the waves silently crash.

Nightdrive

Laurie Bolger

I want to be the girl
in the passenger seat,
feet up on the dashboard
playing with the radio
while you drive

you with one arm around me,
both of us just singing.

Outside the glass is clinging
to a thousand little drops,
I try my best to count them
before the windscreen wipers
quickly flick them off.

I'm watching you
squash your eyelids
at out of date signposts
and neither of us can admit
that we are lost.

Redemption

Marc Swan

for Helen McCrory and Tess Gallagher

If there was a flavour
to the world in which we live
would it be sweet or sour,
have hints of raspberry, lemon,
coffee, fresh mint, a dollop
of salted caramel ice cream
or the tang of dill pickles
for days when all seems far
removed from what we imagine.
Soon the scent of melons
ripening on the vine, strawberries,
sweet and juicy, easy on the tongue.
Lest we forget apples blossoming,
fresh watermelons for the lazy hazy
days of summer. We're in the birth
of another spring flowing
from a hard winter of ice and snow,
and maybe, if we allow it, we'll taste
forgiveness we lost so long ago.

Inside

Laura Treacy Bentley

If winter comes, can spring be far behind?
~Percy Bysshe Shelley

looking out at a classic film noir
with falling snow and dusky alleyways,
I struggle to stay awake
in this black and white scenario.

Church bells toll each hour in the long days
of sameness and slower death.
Masked actors leave the set

for an hour or two,
keeping safe distance.
Everyone is suspect.
When a train thunders by,

I startle awake
and wonder what day it is.
Fumbling for my phone,

I link to an empty Italian cathedral.
A blind man sings *Ave Maria*
to unseen millions.
Then, he walks unaided

down the aisle,
exits through a bronze doorway,
and steps into a watercolour morning.

The man stands alone in Cathedral Square.
His words echo down deserted streets:
"Was blind but now I see."
It feels as if I'm live-streaming

my own funeral, and no one came.
I can't seem to catch
my breath.

Outside now, a motion-detector haloes
a black bear leading her small cubs
across my yard into the shadows.
I raise my window and listen

to a chorus of Spring Peepers
that pulsate the night.
Daffodils bloom bright

under new fallen snow.
A scarlet tanager sings of hope
from the top of a scrub pine.
I wrap myself in a wool blanket

and leave the window open
until first light.

One Day You'll Miss This

Niall Bradley

One day you'll miss this
this sitcom rerun
this house

this life as unexciting as your own touch
as bland and familiar as meeting your own eyes through a mirror
this restaurant blackboard where you write your day

One day you'll miss this
and you might know that
but still it's hard to detach
like something you created and know so well
that saying if it's good or bad
is like trying to know your own scent
like trying to see the back of your own head

One day you'll miss this house
that changes with you
the light switches you can find in the dark
the crannies and flaws you know by name

One day you'll miss them
these people you do not change for

these people you reflect off
like a hall of mirrors
even when those reflections are distorted and magnified
in parts
till you can't recognise yourself
you'll miss them
and these talks you forget as they happen

this life coursing with subtle love

this sitcom rerun
you come back to again
chest swelling in anticipation of the punchline you already know
until you don't laugh but feel safe
to switch off
to voices you know
and conflicts you've seen resolved

One day it will stop
and you won't find the show anywhere
except in screenshots and compilations
the mirror will reflect something else
and in your new life coursing with subtle love
repeat it or you'll forget
one day you'll miss this
one day you'll miss this.

The Big Snow

Colm Scully

Do you remember the Big Snow, I ask?

You remember all of them.

Forty seven,
horses pull coffins over frozen ground,
two weeks before a man can be buried,
the wells frozen, the army tied to barracks
while the turf ran out.
You're at typing school, Miss Lombard's.
Making your way up Patrick's Hill.
Your father's socks pulled over patent pumps,
digging your heels into the ice.
Shorthand copy squeezed under your arm,
dreaming of your first job.

Eighty two,
ESB men out on the pylons,
soldiers deliver water off the back of trucks,
the Commons Road, a hundred metre ski slope
for fertiliser bags and school sacks.
You keep your youngest home,
a housewife twenty years, you hold the house

while we're off playing.
The mobile grocery van arrives
through heavy drifts with spuds and sausages,
your saviour from Fair Hill.

And then the last, 2018.
Schools closed for five days. No bread.
Queues for wine outside the service station.
You phone to tell us 'Stay indoors, don't cross the city.
The roads are treacherous, cars abandoned,
a child was killed in a fall in Farranree.
'Tis worse than forty seven.'
You're nearly ninety, your peers are dead,
you won't see weather like this again.
The slushy mountains thaw to black
along the roadside.

Broken

Billy Fenton

STEVIE SWIPED HIS HAND ACROSS the misted-up window, squinted through the drop of rain, across to the opposite caravan where his best friend Michael lived.

'When will it stop raining?' he said.

Behind him dishes clinked, cupboard doors opened and closed, pop music played on the radio. Stevie's mother hummed along with each tune as she worked.

'When will it stop raining?' he said again, his face now turned in her direction.

'It's getting lighter, Stevie, it shouldn't be long,' she said.

He sighed, leaned his head against his upturned fist, looked at his nails, and started to chew.

'I'm bored out of me head,' he mumbled.

'Stop biting your nails,' his mother said. 'How many times have I told you.'

He wiped the tips of his fingers down the front of his tee shirt.

'Why don't you read one of them?' she said pointing to the scattered pile of comic books on the table. She turned away and continued with her work. Stevie pushed the comics aside and stared through the window.

A few moments later the caravan door opened and his father came in.

'Ah Paddy,' his mother said. 'Wipe your feet, will you.'

She leant down and wiped his boot prints from the floor.

'Come on you,' his father said to Stevie. 'I'm heading up to McGonagle's to sell that load of car batteries. Any chance of a bit of help?'

Stevie loved *McGonagle's Breakers Yard*. It was a field of exotic treasures. All you had to do was ask Ned, the boss man, what you wanted, and he'd disappear into a mass of metal, and re-emerge with the required part. Other times they'd stand by his father's van, and Ned would examine carefully what was for sale, and some words and numbers would be exchanged, and then some cash would change hands and they'd both unload the van. Sometimes their words frightened him. They sounded angry, and occasionally they even banged the side of the van. But they always ended up smiling.

When they reached Garryvoe, a narrow street of houses and shops, two cars were stopped in the centre of the road. The occupants were chatting and laughing to each other and another half-visible figure was crouched down between the two cars. After a few moments Stevie's father's fingers started to tap the steering wheel, and he began to mumble some words which Stevie couldn't make out.

'What are they at?' he finally said.

He moved back and forth in his seat, and the tapping on the steering wheel became more pronounced. Another vehicle pulled up behind them.

'Doesn't he know there's cars waiting?'

He rolled down the window and stuck his head out, and then pushed the horn. Nothing happened, so he pushed it again.

The hunkered-down figure rose and motioned the two cars on, began to walk in their direction, put on a dark cap as he strode.

Stevie's father hit the steering wheel with both hands and said, 'Shit.'

'What's this?' the man said through his teeth as if he was spitting at Stevie's father.

'Sorry, guard,' Stevie's father said. 'I didn't know you was there.'

'Didn't know I was there? Are you blind or what?'

'I only saw two cars blocking the way, guard. Stopped in the middle of the road.'

The guard placed his hand on the door and said, 'Am I hearing right?' and with his other hand he reached up and tugged at his ear.

'No offence meant, boss; it's just what I saw.'

The guard motioned with his head. 'Pull in over there,' he said.

Stevie's father looked at Stevie, exhaled sharply, and jerked the van over to the side of the road.

'Now get out,' the guard said.

Stevie's father opened the door and climbed out of the van.

'Licence?'

'I don't have it with me.'

'What's your name?'

'What did I do, guard?'

'Your name?'

'Paddy Dunne.'

'And where do you live?'

'The halting site in Kildree.'

The guard nodded and said, 'Where are you off to?'

Stevie's father didn't answer immediately and then said, 'McGonagle's breakers yard.'

'What for?'

'To sell some batteries.'

The guard pointed towards the back of the van.

'Open up,' he said.

Stevie couldn't see them as they moved along the side of the van, and he turned around waiting for the back door to open. Their shadows appeared through the grime of the rear window and he could hear angry words passing between them. The back door opened and Stevie saw the twelve batteries lined up in two neat rows along the centre of the van.

'Where did you get these?' the guard said.

'Here and there. I pick them up as I go along,' Stevie's father said.

'As you go along?'

The guard poked his head into the back of the van, lifted a tarpaulin that was crumpled up along the side, threw it up towards the front of the van. He caught Stevie's eye.

Stevie stared back at him. 'Me Daddy did nothing wrong,' he said. The guard stood back up at the rear of the van so that Stevie could only see the lower part of their bodies.

'Me Daddy did nothing wrong,' he shouted.

The back door slammed shut and Stevie could no longer see them.

He thought of getting out, but before he could, his father climbed back in, and they moved quickly out on to the road.

'You did nothing wrong, Daddy,' Stevie said.

He glanced at Stevie sideways, shook his head.

Stevie turned towards the side window, the outside world turning into a blur of grey through tears that were starting to form. He managed to hold most of them back. He didn't want his father to see him crying, wiped away what he could with the sleeve of his jacket.

His father drove faster than usual as they continued on their way towards Ned's. A few times the van scraped the branches on the hedgerows.

Finally, up ahead Stevie could make out the mass of coloured metal that was Ned's, and he began to forget, and he thought of how he'd examine and sit in the cars that had arrived since his last visit.

When they pulled in the gate was shut.

'What's going on?' Stevie's father said.

He got out of the van and walked up to the gate, pushed it hard, but it wouldn't move. Stevie got out, followed him as he walked towards the house.

There was no one in.

'That's odd. I hope they're all right.'

His father walked to a window and looked in, raised his hand to his face to shade his eyes.

He began to walk back towards the van. Stevie didn't follow. Instead, his eyes traced the outlines of reds and greens, and all the other colours that filled the yard behind the barbed wire fence. Ned's dog poked its head through and whined. Two cars he hadn't seen before were parked inside the gate.

'Come on, Stevie.'

'No,' Stevie cried. 'No.'

'Come on!'

Stevie shook his head.

He heard the gravel crunch as his father walked back towards him.

'No!' he repeated.

Stevie reached down, took up a fistful of chippings from the driveway, and threw it hard at Ned's front wall. Reached down and threw another. A few of the stones bounced off the window, leaving behind a crack in the glass. His father's hand came down with a slap on the back of Stevie's head. Stevie stumbled sideways. When he looked back, his father's eyes were filling with tears and he turned away.

'Why did you do that?' his father said. 'Why?'

The Women Who Are Dead

Jane Burn

Each of the times that I have been alive each of the women
that swung upon my bones   each age each clumsy bloom
kept beneath the barrow of my skin for there must be a place
to hallow what is left   I made my heart into a charnel house

the women who are dead will always need a place to still
their used and shacky selves I laid these moon-faced hulls
into their own quiet shaft the kinds of me that there has been
made a keepsake of each ounce of blood each different limb

Baby/me quiet inside her wicker crib little bloom of flesh
a cloistered gem a cradle's cap of euphoric smell Baby/me knew
only small needs of milk and sleep lengthenings of arm and foot
expansions of mouth and eye   ideas of face and light

Childhood/me offered to the catacombs of school inchoate
against the playground's bruise was haunted by the warped home
of someone else's clothes   flailed at grammar's daunting plagues
Childhood/me learned the shame of manifold tongues

Daughter/me   was not the right child   not good as gold
her name a hex   a strange bird vent from the cree
of her own mother's lips   Daughter/me   a bad gift of screams
scratched at the walls for her changeling self

Vitiated/me   mouthed like sin through a confessor's grille
witness to a transgression of spires   the truculence of hands
the vile of milt and iron   debitage upon the puckered bed
Vitiated/me   shaped into grief by evil blades

Wedded/me   tulle ghost   led along an artery of stones
curing peevish days with pliant smiles   maundering at cupboards
raking a drawer's noise of spoons and forks   Wedded/me   peon
to a wall's pool of unrelenting time   had a throat of pearls

Mother/me   resting palms upon a crucible womb   afflictions
of slack and brindled skin   brooking every livid welt of pain
the glad insomnolence   Mother/me   curator of deciduous teeth
discovering   the sweet knife of a young spine

Sonnet 4

Ray Malone

there then in the grass that day breath to breath
hills away from here eyes and minds mingling
hearts too who knows who paused to measure pulse
to the ears of blood the numberless beats

who held harboured there in the green embrace
thought of an end then of an estuary
of all but a flood of infinity
of minutes gone on to past hours to come

who felt bound to abide the beat of sun
the height of its now then the heat of it
breast to breast in the blue lost to the press
of all but earth and the urge to enter there

the brief trace of now that day there in the grass
that breach of green its bruised remembering

Her Soul to Keep

Steve Wade

THE PROPERTY, A LARGE THREE-STOREY Georgian house, secretly owned by her newly deceased husband, by default, was now hers.

At first Sally wanted nothing to do with it. Figured she'd just sell it. But her brother convinced her to hold on to it. He told her the time wasn't right. Nobody was buying. Better to move in for a year or so until the market picked up. So she did.

A couple of weeks before Christmas, Sally sold their two-bedroomed semi-detached, bought a Polo estate car and took up residence with her three, now fatherless, children. That her husband was dead, she sometimes found hard to accept. That he had been leading a double life with a second wife and child filled her with outrage. But the details of how he ended his own life, and the lives of the other woman and the woman's little boy, left her terrified.

But somehow the confused anger and horror at what he'd done gave her the resilience to carry on. Besides, the boys, seven-year-old Ash, and the four-year old twins, Dillon and Rafferty, needed her. Her parental duties had now doubled.

Almost eighteen months back now, since she first told them that Daddy had gone away. The twins didn't get it, of course. While Ash seemed old enough to understand, but too young to really take in the emotional impact of no longer having a father. But, although he never openly cried, he did become a tad morose. And he spoke less than he once had. He engrossed himself in his Boogie Board writing tablet, his Flip to Win Hangman game, and his Roald Dahl books.

The new house, for the boys, was one big playground. With its indoor, heated swimming pool, its high-ceilinged rooms with wooden floors, a viewing tower, and an enclosed courtyard, Sally wished that she too could have been a child. Because then she wouldn't have had to deal with the house's recent history.

For this was the place where he – she no longer wanted to even think his name – put a double-barrel shotgun to the other woman's head on a Saturday morning. And then ran from the room and met their five-year-old son running towards him from his own room. At least this is how the police detectives examining the crime scene, along with the state pathologist, had pieced it together. The boy had probably been woken by the gunfire. Sally always tried to avoid visualising graphically the end to the little boy's short life. She skipped to her husband reloading the weapon, flipping it upside down and placing the muzzle beneath his own chin and squeezing the trigger.

And so it was natural that Sally felt terribly uneasy on moving into what the locals called 'The House of Horrors'. A house from whose upstairs windows a ghostly white figure of a woman had been seen crying in the night. Not that Sally had time for such superstitious or misguided beliefs. But how else was she going to feel in a house where such an unspeakable onslaught had occurred?

From the first day she stepped over the threshold into the Georgian house with its original stonework, Sally sensed something that she had never before felt. Far colder than outdoors, the cold burrowed under her flesh and into her bones. It made her teeth chatter. The twins, who initially clung to her coat, realised that they too could make their teeth clack by just opening their mouths and copying their mom. This was fun.

Even when she got the heat turned on, there were areas in the house which remained Arctic. Perhaps the underfloor heating system was faulty in those parts of the house. Particularly cold was the hall where her husband's child had died. And, of course, the landing was the one outside the bedrooms of the mother and the child. Rooms Sally ensured were at all times locked.

The bedrooms Sally chose for herself and the children were on a different floor, the one beneath the one where her husband had carried out his horrific attack. The boys, she decided, to begin with, would stay with her in her room. She had ordered in three single beds accordingly. Not that she believed they were in any danger but having them close to her at night-time was comforting. For her, she had to admit, more than for them.

To begin with, everything was fine at bedtime. The twins, Dillon and Rafferty, played computer games for a bit, while Ash usually got lost in his Roald Dahl books. But as soon as they were asleep, Sally began to sense another presence or other presences in the house besides theirs. Coming from the bedroom walls a scratching sound. Probably tiny mice paws or rodent teeth, but her imagination suggested something else. And then there were voices, muffled voices screaming, as though from behind closed doors. But this could just have been her disturbed imagination. Something that insinuated itself into those confused and confusing periods between wakefulness and sleep.

The boys, however, seemed to experience no such anxieties. Rafferty did continue to speak in his sleep. But this was something he had been doing long before any of this happened. And he sounded no worse than he had before. Perhaps he may have even improved a bit, for he no longer slipped into her bed in the middle of the night. For this Sally was relieved. Her role was now to prepare them for adulthood, to fill their childhood years with as many happy and positive memories as possible. Memories that might help to temper the awfulness of being abandoned by their daddy. But Sally's already challenging role became even more difficult on the night of December 21st, the shortest day and the longest night of the year.

Stirred into drowsy wakefulness from an unusually deep sleep by the familiar feel of Rafferty slipping into the bed next to her, she put her arm about him and drew him to her. With the usual, steady realisation of where she was, and what had happened over the past year, the feel of her son's body and his sweet milky odour calmed her. That he had reverted to old habits didn't matter. She had a purpose. She was meant to be. It made her feel so worthy to be alive. With the contentment that came with this understanding, she drifted back to sleep.

Sometime later, Sally felt herself being once more pulled from sleep. She kept her eyes closed and listened. Rafferty. He was talking in his sleep again. His words were mostly mumbles intertwined with confused phrases and exclamations: 'Santa Claus. Rice krispies. Daddy. A rainbow. Grandad and Granny.' And replacing the milky scent of his skin was a faint fragrance of lilies and the dankness of wet earth.

As Sally's senses became clearer, an invisible hand, it felt like, grasped her stomach from the inside. Rafferty's voice was coming from his own bed. Her body tensed. And the child next to her, over whose body her arm was draped, giggled a breathy giggle. Not Dillon's or Ash's giggle. She squeezed tighter her closed eyes. To open them now would be to witness in the subdued light something for which she was unprepared. For which she had no reference.

Instead she resorted to something she hadn't done for so long. She began to pray. To recite words that she once believed in. That, as a child, helped her fight away the thoughts of the bogeyman behind the wardrobe. But through her own manic praying, the child's voice piped up.

'Mama,' it said.

Sally felt her entire body react. She needed to relieve herself and was nauseated at the one time. She prayed louder and tried to ease away from the thing next to her, but it turned to her. She could feel it shifting. And on her face, she felt its soft breath.

'Mama.'

'Yes,' she heard her own voice say in a timbre that belonged to someone else.

'Do the down to sleep one, Mama.'

'What?' she said.

'Down to sleep,' it repeated.

She listened as the thing beside her tried to recite what she recognised as Psalm 4:8 from the Old Testament.

'Okay,' she said, not sure if this were all some awful nightmare, or if she had finally gone completely under. *'Now I lay me down to sleep, I pray the Lord my soul to keep. Angels watch me through the night ...'*

The sound of what had to be a gunshot caused her to let out a scream in a pitch she had never before made. But the scream sounded only in her head.

'Mama,' the child beside her shouted, as she felt and heard him leap from the bed, his little feet pattering from the room. 'Mama, Mama.'

Sally sat up and opened her eyes when the child was out of the room. A subliminal sweep of the boys' beds reassured her that none of them had awoken or was aware of anything outside his own dreams. With her hand clamped to her own mouth, she heard a voice with which she was familiar. Her dead husband's voice. Though he sounded highly agitated. The hysterical screaming of the child for his mama mingled with the man shouting at the boy.

'No. Come here,' he said. 'Turn around. Don't look at me. Look. Look there. At the crib.' His words were interspersed with demented sobs. Sally could picture him trying to twist the terrified child about by the shoulders, so he didn't have to look into his petrified eyes.

And then another shot rang out. But not the loud crack of movies, where the sound echoes through a valley. It sounded more muffled, like someone bursting a balloon. And then silence. The boy's screams cut off as though he had been unplugged.

There came then a long, drawn-out roar from her dead husband. A sound that had behind it a huge intake of breath. Sally knew what came next. She heard him popping the empty cartridges and replacing them. She waited. But the third shot didn't come. Instead, she saw his shadow slip under the half-open bedroom door. And the sound of the door brushing the carpet as it began to move slowly inwards.

Sally squeezed her eyes shut and clamped her palms over them. She could sense him in the room now. His heavy, rank, male odour far stronger than it ever was. And his breathing, loud and angry, completed the image that would never leave her alone: a nostril flaring, blood-spattered, gun-wielding killer, with a singular drive – to satiate his perverted lust to kill.

Unbidden, the lines came from her in a manic mantra: *'If I die before I wake, I ask the Lord my soul to take. If I die before I wake, I ask the Lord my soul to take. If I die before I ...'*

The loud bang of the third gunshot outside the bedroom door resounded in her chest. She screamed aloud, which woke the boys. And they in turn screamed and shouted, as they jumped from their beds and scrambled in beside her, burrowing under the duvet.

As best she could, Sally tried to calm them. Although her own voice sounded anything but calm.

'It was just a dream,' she said, stroking their tiny shapes beneath the red and white duvet. 'Mommy just had a bad dream, is all.'

The first to pop out his head was Ash, on his face a big smile. Dillon and Rafferty followed him in unison, the way they did everything. Their tearful faces turned to giggles and they hugged her, one each side of her neck. Ash giggled too. But then another giggle came from the end of the bed. Sally dropped her eyes to a fourth figure hidden beneath the duvet. The boys' heads turned too.

Firefly

Susan Richardson

You are the nucleus of a spark
setting fire to dogwood,
a leaf on the wind,
soaring into the arms of a river,
raging in the belly of the moon.

When I say I want you to love me,
I mean I want to be captured,
buried in the eye of your storm.
I want to be the gun strapped to your hip,
swallow your unrelenting grit.

When I am wild eyed and craving you,
pull me across murky boundaries,
touch me like you mean it,
leave me in disarray.

When you no longer feel my touch
firm against your holster,
when you strain to hear my yearning,
don't hesitate,
be quick to pluck out my tongue.

I will become the wind

Promise you won't inhale me,
until time restores my wings
and the sky is ours for the taking.

Bats

Liz Byrne

If I could be that small,
I would fit inside a crack in the tree's bark
with my others.

A crowd of us
could become tree, safe for the bright daylight hours
or dark or winter.

We could be cloud,
a colony to roost, birth and raise our young,
alone and together.

We could fly at dusk,
not a bird but a stitching of the sky in a dance
of dart and swoop.

I could send my voice
to bounce off telephone wires and sound out my others,
a language too high for humans to hear.

I could hang upside-down
like a scrap of tattered leather; be a story
of sucking blood, vampires, Dracula.

If I could be
that other to myself and to you,
I might feel safe.

Basso Profundo

Maeve Reilly

Some dawn, some fogged
October morning after first frost
after you've lain a long time alone
primed by silence
for the faintest footfall
you will hear the earth turning
the unmistakable scrape
of iron, of rock, that shale
that hauls the not yet counted day
over the curved land.

The floor beneath your floor
will shudder with earth's exertion
to keep its course –
is it ark or terra firma
that carries our freight –
once tilted godward,
now away?

Some dawn, some fogged
October morning after first frost
the world will strike
you like a tuning fork,
you will bear the seismic clash
of falling leaf on grass,
earth's hoarse boding
last ditch chantey
orbits closing.

The Nights Are Long

Hugo Kelly

MY WIFE SLEEPS HER MEDICATED SLEEP, a sullen state that cannot be broken bar loud explosions or the occasional chemical nightmare that causes her to cry out like a young girl. It is in these moments that I think that I still love her. I slip out of the marital bed, leave its fleshy warmth and go downstairs through the maze of shadows. The house vibrates from our industrial fridge in the kitchen, humming like a giant battery.

In the study next to the kitchen I leave the light off, preferring the darkness. Picking up the phone I press the first few digits of the number, counting each one with deliberation as if I am entering a secret code. But then inexplicably I hesitate. I carefully replace the receiver.

I am not ready. No. Not yet.

Back in the kitchen, I survey the neat worktop and shining silver of our appliances. My head throbs with the gritty presence of insomnia and my mouth is dry. The light pours into the kitchen from our neighbour's sensor lights that turn the four-bedroomed house into a labour camp, circa 1950s Siberia. I stare out into the ferocious brightness and see that the back window of the house behind us is also lit and that there is a woman standing within its frame looking out. We both stare at each other, and I raise a hand and wave to her. Comically she lifts a stiff arm and waves to me in return. Then she pulls the curtains closed. Within seconds the sensor lights go out. A suburban darkness falls again.

I turn on the tap and pour myself a glass of water and drink it back. I am caught between actions and that tension causes my arid mind to ache more. I put down the glass and walk briskly back into my study. My hand hovers above the phone but this time I grip it firmly and dial the number. I can imagine its noise breaking the silence of night in her house. I think of her being roused from her bed. I think about the doubt and fear that such intrusions cause. The burr of the phone rings in my ear. She waits beside the phone but does not pick up.

The phone rings out.

I dial the number again.

Her name is Catherine. We met one afternoon in our underused municipal gallery. She has fine dark brown hair and an oval shaped face resistant to the effects of the middle years. It was her faint knowing smile, an expression of bemused intelligence, which won me over. We chatted about the work on display, a video piece by a Japanese-American artist where men cycled forlornly under the green-tinted sea between the outcrops of a rocky reef.

'It is beautiful,' she said, 'but also a bit troubling.'

'Yes,' I agreed, though the work had made little impression on me.

Later we went to the small gallery restaurant, a useful place for such meetings, and afterwards I asked her for her phone number. She hesitated and then gave it to me.

'I don't normally do this,' she said.

Don't worry, I thought, I do.

We met three times in the following fortnight and then one weekday when the rest of the world was busy, we went to my room on the Western Road that I rent by the week. It is in a large, detached house, built with bullish optimism in the wrong place at the wrong time. It is now mostly populated by Polish and Lithuanian workers and the odd anomaly like me who comes and goes without any obvious routine. There we lay huddled on the bare sheets as the muffled transient sounds crouched around us and talked with the honesty that such brief affairs entice. Afterwards she put on her jacket and smoothed back her long hair.

'This is over now,' she said. 'I won't see you again. It's for the best.'

At the time I said nothing, but I knew I could not accept this.

It's just the way I am.

The phone rings dead. I suck in another breath of dead air and then type the numbers again. The phone burrs once and is suddenly answered.

Her harried breathing foretells anger.

'You promised you wouldn't keep ringing,' she says. 'You promised you would leave me alone.'

'I know.'

'You promised.'

'I know,' I reply.

'This isn't right ...' she says. 'It isn't fair.'

I don't deny this. I know that it isn't.

From somewhere there is the gurgling of pipes. The fridge shudders. A boy racer accelerates in the distance. The gloss of silence shines again. Her breathing has returned to normal. It usually does.

'My husband is suspicious,' she says.

'Your husband works nights,' I state.

'He might ring for something, and the phone would be engaged.'

'There's no need to be so dramatic.'

'I don't understand this,' she says. 'I don't understand what you want from me.'

'I want to see you again. I think you gave up too easily.'

'No,' she says. 'Just no.'

'I am trying to be reasonable,' I say. 'I miss meeting you at the gallery. Did you go to Dublin to see the Turner sketches as you said you would?'

'No,' she says and does not elaborate further.

'Tell me about your day.'

'I will ring the guards. I don't care anymore.'

A floorboard creaks overhead. I gaze at the ceiling. Catherine is angry at me. I have failed. Like I failed with the others. But still I continue.

'I think I love you,' I say. 'I just had to tell you that.'

'No,' she says. 'You don't love me. You just don't. This isn't about love. Love is the *last thing* that this is about.'

I don't contradict her.

And then I hear a soft sobbing.

'I am a good person,' she says. 'I don't deserve this.'

'You are a good person,' I say. 'I am sorry that you are upset.'

She exhales forcefully. The phone clicks to silence. I put the receiver down. I turn and walk across the cold tiles until I come to the stairs and ponderously walk up. The paintings on the walls are ghostly spectres staring at me.

In the spare room I stare out on the dark houses of the estates spread out compact and neat like the dusty letters of a forgotten keyboard, so new and yet already so useless. The night sky is swept with fragmentary cloud and the thin distant light of the stars is just visible. I place my fingertips on the cool glass of the window and press until the skin feels numb. I know that I will ring her again. I know that I will not be able to stop myself.

Back in my marriage bed I settle once again in its earthy warmth. My wife snores gently. How will I change, I wonder. This behaviour can't go on. But I do not know how to stop. My wife will find out. One day there will be a guard at the door. There will be questions that I cannot answer. There will be guilt. A lone tear squeezes from my eye, a drop of acid burning the white tissue. So, the minutes pass and I ask myself again why I am this person. But I do not know the answer. And I know sleep will not come to release me from this question.

My Mother as St. Perpetua

Bryce Emley

and I obtained leave for my baby to remain in the prison with me ... and my prison suddenly became a palace to me, and I would rather have been there than anywhere else
— St. Perpetua, from *Passio SS. Perpetuae et Felicitas*

I believed a mother's gift
            was not her child, but her capacity

    to release him from her sadness.
I swear I felt you everywhere,

            even in my loneliness. No,
    especially in my loneliness.

My child, my regret has been belief
            in one who would ask for us to give to him

    what we couldn't live without.
And if I could do it again, I would.

            And if I could do it again,
    I would find another offering than us.

The Arborist's Wife

Cheryl Pearson

On our wedding night he melted my dress clean off –
long column of silk like a candle puddled pale at my ankles.
Back then he loved the black-pepper freckles along my spine,
the webs of skin between my toes; every sun-shy part of me.
I should have married a trawlerman instead, glad for the dry
harbour of my arms. An arborist's head is in the clouds. How
can I compete? The clean air, the green-gold light. All that sturdy
beauty. My thighs dimple like fruit-peel. My cleavage hangs
like a cow's. A daughter would have sweetened my arms. A son.
I counted six summers, no children. These days St Monica
hangs from my neck, patron saint of home-makers, difficult
marriages. I lay the table with fine china. One plate. One saucer.
He murmurs sweet nothings to his poplar. I peg his wet shirts
to the line, startle the hares. Like him they run from me to her.

Tanuki

Jessamyn Fairfield

It was late in the year
to find a wagtail so small.
White and black feathers around
wide yellow eyes,
as if asking a question.
Sweetling, who followed
the light of the autumn moon
into our window,
our warm home
in the lengthening nights.
An old blue shirt became
a bed, until he discovered
the warmth of the clothes
we wore, curled in a hood or
under a sweater.
The discovery that I too
carried someone small inside me –
the two of them together, hearing
each other coo through my hot skin.
Feathers staying longer and longer.
We looked for answers, changed
food, water, and watched.
What we took for affection

eventually turned to lethargy,
an affection of drowning.
The rain stayed off him
but he curled into
near loss, miraculous recovery –
our wildling survived the solstice
hibernating with us.
Days later, stiff and cold
in the soft old shirt
we found him.
Still in shock,
Clutching him to my chest.
The tree and tinsel are gone now,
And he is back in the garden.
The damp soft earth can hold
What my blood could not –
The care and the grieving.

Jenny Greenteeth

Estelle Price

Her womb bulges with duckweed and grief –
Jenny bog-hag, woman of green skin, green teeth,
lurking in the reeds, hair tangled, long arms poised
to tug at a child's thin ankles. She keeps the moss
under siege, floats a lullaby up to the birches,
her eyes, two suns flecked with cerise. Watch out,
watch out for your babies. She's turning about.
She's the sudden mist on the moor, the car door
flung open, the riptide rocking a daughter out to sea.
So desperate she – for a child. She'll take one anyhow.
She's the woman who miscarried, stole a newborn
from Maternity. She's Jenny and she's me, peering
into prams, Old Mother Hubbard gloating in our dreams –
see how we lie, lost in the crib of make-believe.

A Bigger Boat

Feargal Ó Dubhghaill

THERE IT IS, THE DOORBELL'S RINGING. Mary's in the kitchen, asks me to get it.

As I get up from the armchair, I remind myself of the name. Ciara Ann. *Ciara Ann Magennis.* Michael spelt it out for us on the phone. *C-i-a-r-a, Ann* without an *'e', 'M-a-g-e-n-n-i-s'*. A Northerner. You'd have to be with a name like that.

But this could be something. It's a long time since Michael brought a woman over. Michael is forty-five. We would like to see our first-born settle down.

Have to say I'm a bit nervous. But I should just be myself. We should be ourselves.

I pin back my shoulders, take a quick look in the hall mirror, then go and open the front door. And there they are. Michael's well turned out, in jeans and a smart check shirt. And Ciara Ann, she's a fine-looking girl, dark hair and in a long summery dress. She looks a lot younger than Michael, which I have to admit I'm pleased about.

In Michael's right hand is a bottle of whiskey, in his left a bunch of flowers. So thoughtful of them both.

Michael hands me the whiskey and hugs me. These days it's all hugs when we meet. It's his idea, maybe it's to do with everyone getting older. Then Mary emerges from the kitchen, all smiles, apologising for her damp hands. She beams at the flowers, says they shouldn't have, they really shouldn't have.

After the hugs and handshakes, I show our guests to the sitting room and tell them dinner will be ready soon. I offer them a drink.

Both ask for only water. A bit unexciting, if you ask me, but I get them their water. Plenty of it in the tap.

'So,' I ask, 'how was your weekend?' Good question for a bank holiday Monday, eh?

'Great.' That's Ciara Ann speaking. God that *is* a strong accent. *Greeyet.* Sounds like Bernadette Devlin sometime around 1969 on a crackly TV and the Bogside erupting. The North. It all looked so far away but it was nearer than you thought.

Ciara Ann looks at Michael, as though to invite him to speak.

'Great, thanks,' Michael says.

That's all he says. Can you credit that? The man's a high-flying solicitor, usually never stuck for words, and that's all he says. How's he going to impress this lady if he leaves it to his elderly father to keep the chat flowing?

'And how was yours?' It's Ciara Ann.

She's asking me?

'How was *your* weekend?' she asks again, all smiles. Looks like she really wants to know.

Eh?

Just then Mary pokes her head in from the kitchen and rescues me.

'I'm going to borrow Tom a moment,' she explains to our guests. 'Then we'll be ready.'

Out in the kitchen I slice the beef as Mary sorts the vegetables. And I think about Ciara Ann's question, the one asking us about our weekend. I mean, for Mary and me, at this stage of our lives, sure isn't every day just like the next, weekend or not? Outside of Sunday Mass together, Mary does her thing and I do mine.

I bring the dinner plates into the dining room and I see that Michael and Ciara Ann are already seated at the table. Oh?

'This is wonderful,' says Ciara Ann, her eyes sweeping the room. 'Thank you so much for having us.'

There. She's doing the talking again, talking for the two of them. Mary won't like that. But, you know what, I think Michael, maybe more than other lads, needs a woman to, well, keep him right. It's not like there hasn't been a few of them along the way. There's been plenty, and you'd just ask yourself why he couldn't stay with any of them. Now, I don't want to be making comparisons, but with Mary and me it just seemed right from the very beginning. Walked her home from a rugby club dance. Asked if I could see her again. She made me wait three days. We're together ever since.

*

As we sit to table, Mary says grace. Grace before meals is sacrosanct in this house, visitors or not. There can be no apology for thanking the Lord for a good repast.

I ask Ciara Ann what wine she would like.

'I'd love a red,' she says straight away.

'Good,' I say. 'I've a fine fruity one here. One of my favourites.'

Mary will have the same, but Michael goes for the water again. 'Designated driver,' he says. I know better than to argue.

The four of us clink glasses. 'To togetherness,' I say, why not? To togetherness.

As we tuck in, we chit-chat about the weather, and what's on TV. Harmless stuff, barely a mention of politics or anything. We find out that Ciara Ann is a teacher. I like that. I'd hate to see Michael with another lawyer. They're both looking happy and I know Mary's thinking what I'm thinking.

'So,' Mary asks, 'how did this love story begin?'

Nice one, the way she's posed it, throwing it out to the two of them.

'An act of charity,' Michael chuckles, pouring gravy over his beef.

Oh?

Then Ciara Ann jumps in. 'It was a fundraiser, a quiz,' she says. God, listen to that accent. *A quaz.* 'A big one,' she says, 'maybe fifty tables, teams of four, and we found ourselves lumped in together.'

A bag one. Faftih teeyebles.

'I arrived late,' says Michael, glancing at her. 'All the solicitors' tables were full, so they put me in with three teachers.'

'And how did you do in the quiz?' I ask, maybe too curiously.

'Oh,' says Michael nonchalantly. 'Creditably enough.' Such a lawyer's answer, giving nothing away.

'Och, I think we let Michael down,' says Ciara Ann, flicking back some wisps of hair from her face. She turns to Michael. 'Remember the one about the boat?'

The boat?

Michael grins, then frowns. 'Oh yeah?' Looks like he doesn't want to, eh, go there. So Ciara Ann speaks again.

'There was this question,' she says, 'about this quote from a movie, the quote was "*we're gonna need a bigger boat*". We had to name the movie.'

The way she says it, "*we're gonna need a bigger boat*", it sounds a bit scary. Then she starts to giggle.

'Michael knew the answer,' she says.

Michael looks at us both. 'Do you guys know the answer?' he asks.

You guys!

'The answer to what?' I ask.

'That question,' he says. 'About the name of the movie. The movie that that line is taken from.'

'"*We're gonna need a bigger boat*",' Mary mouths the words slowly. Funny to hear Mary saying something like that. This Ciara Ann seems to have put everyone on the spot.

I haven't a clue what the answer is. I'm too old for this. Michael and Ciara Ann look at us, Ciara Ann's face full of divilment. I see that by now everyone has finished dinner. Isn't it time for dessert?

Mary's face brightens. 'Was it *Titanic*?' she asks. Mary's being a good sport, more power to her.

But *Titanic*, yes. Sounds to me like a fair answer. Then I see Ciara Ann's reaction.

'*Titanic!*' she almost screams, then doubles up in laughter, cupping her mouth like a child would, and she turns to Michael, her hair all over the place. '*Titanic!* That's hilarious!'

My toes curl. Such rudeness. Hilarious, how are ya? But Michael's laughing too. Whose side is he on?

'Sorry, Mary!' Ciara Ann says urgently. 'Can I call you Mary?' She knows she's overstepped the mark. '*Titanic* is the answer I had too,' she explains, a bit breathless now. 'And my two friends were sure that was the answer. But his nibs knew better.' She playfully punches Michael on the shoulder, then asks him, 'do you want to tell it?'

'No,' he smiles. 'You have the floor.' And he gently clears more hair from her eyes.

At this I glance at Mary, but she seems not to notice.

'And what was the answer, Michael?' I ask him.

'*Jaws*,' says Michael.

Jaws.

'The one about the shark,' Michael explains.

Ah yes, the one about the shark. *Jaws*, God that's an old one now. I glance again at Mary. When we were younger we would have gone to the pictures a bit. We loved the pictures. But would I have taken her to something like that? I'd say not.

'A shark?' Mary asks.

'Yes, Ma,' says Michael. 'A man-eating shark.'

'Holy moly,' says Mary.

'Surely you heard of *Jaws*, Ma?' says Michael.

'Holy moly,' says Mary a second time. 'And the quote was, again?'

'"*We're gonna need a bigger boat*",' says Ciara Ann. I'd prefer if she'd let Michael say it.

'God!' says Mary. 'And it's about a man-eating shark. That's creepy, isn't it?'

My dear wife, all she wants is for our son to find the right woman, just like our two younger lads did. She couldn't give two hoots about who answered what in a quiz. Right now I just want to put my arm around her, let her know it's all grand, it doesn't matter.

At that moment, Michael reaches out to Mary, puts his hand on hers. 'Don't worry, Ma,' he says, '*Titanic* was a good answer too.' Now there's class.

But Ciara Ann isn't finished. 'Anyway,' she says, 'so there we were at the quiz, three of us teachers and we're all too young to remember *Jaws*, so we think the answer is *Titanic*, and there's this solicitor, this older man, may I say that?' – she turns to Michael – 'and he's insisting that the answer is *Jaws*.'

'I wasn't *insisting*!' Michael protests. Well, sort of a pretend protest.

'And you were right,' says Ciara Ann. Then she looks at Mary and me. 'But do you know what we did?' She threatens to laugh again. 'We voted on it. And Michael was outvoted three to one. So the answer we put down was *Titanic*.'

'Which was the wrong answer,' says Michael, sort of playfully. He's enjoying all this.

'It was,' says Ciara Ann, her hand now touching his. In front of us too. She *does* like him. 'But at least', she says, turning to him, 'you're a good democrat.' He grins.

A gud damocrat. I can see her with a megaphone. And him listening on with admiration.

So there you have it, there's how this love story began. Not exactly *Wuthering Heights*, is it? But I say nothing.

'OK,' says Mary. I think Mary's had enough. 'Now who's for apple crumble?'

'I think that'll get a unanimous vote,' says Michael. Ah. I've always liked his wit.

Mary heads out to the kitchen. Michael gathers the dinner plates and follows her. Ciara Ann excuses herself, goes off to powder her nose.

I stay sitting. Have to say she's a lively lady, this Ciara Ann, no shrinking violet. Asking us about our weekend. As though we'd be out gallivanting.

But each to their own, I suppose. And if they're happy together ... sure that's the main thing, isn't it?

Isn't that all we would want for them? That they would be – well – as happy as we are?

*

And it's got me thinking, you know, wouldn't it be nice if Mary and I went out to the pictures? God knows when we last went. There must be *some* good ones. Why don't we go some night?

I'm going to ask her, that's what I'm going to do. I'm sure she'd like to go. Wouldn't she? Or would she think I've gone nuts? Sure how will I know if I don't ask? Even just to be out together, come to think of it. Like we used to do.

I'll ask her maybe tonight, after we've said goodbye to Michael and his girlfriend. Tonight, when we'll have something to talk about. Tonight, when it'll be just the two of us again.

Confluence

Rebecca Gethin

After rain, where two rivers join
I watch currents hooshing
one coiled inside the other
like lovers spooning.

The swimming in me longs to sleek
between the waterweaving.
Somewhere in that inbetween
must be a slit. If I stand in water

long enough, praying like St Cuthbert,
two otters may warm my feet.
They'll tingle me into paw and layers
of fur, making me undrownable.

I'll learn to whisker fish movements
in the vaults of boulders.
I'll eel through this hubblegush
somersault through spirals

snout among the roaring bubbles.
Later, you may call across the river for me
Dratsie, Uther, Ótr, Water Dog
as if a name could call me back.

The Cailleach

Jean O'Brien

... Winter of age which overwhelms everyone, its first months have come to me
The Lament of the Hag of Beare.

It is January. The Wolf Moon howls yellow
in stormy skies, we need new speech and search
for other words, look for new utterances to soothe
and smooth the twisted tongue, the honeyed hook.

Today I woke and said my morning greetings
in the shower-steamed mirror, my face a ghostly pall
as hooded features emerge from the mist, deep runnels
run from nose to chin, jaw slack with use, time spoils all.

Now I see more within my inner eye, than outer,
I have lost sight of colour, while inside me a riot still runs.
I look for nuggets of language to tell of this new midden,
filled with stones, animal bones, lithics, shells
and all the detritus we leave behind, rattling waymarks.
We lurch on, panning for who knows what.

My spine is a stony cluster burial mound as I jostle for place,
my head a jutting headland, my slack jaw houses a howling skull,
I live within the penumbra of a solar eclipse, our weaponed words
are wintering in the northern hemisphere.
The wolves ride the wind with me,
my hammer, big as Thor's, clatters across the skies.

The Cailleach is a divine hag associated with the creation of landscape and storms.

Hobbling Away From The Sun

Stephen Glennon

I worry about the end of things
yet waste time watching TV re-runs
staying up late in search of lost feelings
sleeping on long after light wakes
rise to spend the day procrastinating

I walk behind a shortened shadow
darkened as the habitual frown
stretched across furrowed brow
its hollow gait no longer hopeful
hobbling away from the sun
the creature always one step ahead

I weigh uneasy rhythms against metronome
envy the musicality of synchronicity
steady silence between heart beats
there is no dance or war of words
just perfect harmony – a reminder
each day to be present and live a little

Respite for a Single Mother

Mary Mullen

i m Matthew Sweeney

She brought forgiveness to the cave
some Lucille Clifton poetry
a small blue generator powered
by unheard good wishes
and pepper to keep grizzlies out.
She dressed her willow bed
with seaweed and cumulus pillows;
she brought sandstorms into the cave,
hushed them down. Quietened everything.
In the melon light she shaped and stitched
a lusty, silky gown in turquoise;
wore it to her willow bed. Aspen trees
outside the cave quivered soft jazz
while she slept like a teenager.
She dreamt of the legend of a *beautiful*
Sioux woman in her cave who wove a rug
with porcupine quills; and of her dog who
ate the quills so the rug would not be finished
and the world would not end.

The Derryquay Meander

Noel King

IT WAS THE BEACH THAT DID IT. His arm enfolding her, then unfolding when people appeared on the horizon. The sand weave has worked in paths that are wordless, invisible paths grafting their love. It was only sand to her before now, sand that broke underfoot, intermittent by silence, a weave, a path she walked back over, the same steps since childhood. Darkness follows her with him now, darkness cooling the sand, dimming the day.

He didn't speak to her again until night had pitched itself at an even keel. It was just to tell her again he loved her, over and over. Quaint, she thought, he had to wait for night's blanket. Perhaps he feared light was a bearer of secrets?

Dull white lights from the village street had showed them their way to the beach. If they walked a little further, they would hit caravan park lights, the odd cry of a baby, a fight of a family carrying out into the stillness. A little way back would mean again the sound of a pub, the people they've left there; a sing-song ding-dong they both realised they hated.

Still, he seems to lead on and on; just a way, any way, a route was irrelevant, she trusts his instincts, knows she will be safe from the sea. She has never been safe from circumstances that have made her, over thirty-four years, what she is; until he spoke to her by the fireplace in that big pub; a summer pub, it's grate a clutter of sweet papers, ashes, tissues. Neither knew they could be searching to find a place with another. He led a way away from a flutter of babble inside, separated her from the group, led her here to *his* island, made it *their* island.

He has made himself a home in her ear. She becomes aware of her feet getting cold, but trusts his lead, uncomplaining. The voice she hears soothes the blisters of past lovers, sore spots where she thought she could never love again. His words are only of soft memories, childhood beaches. None of that is very important, yet every word she wants to remember. She must keep reminding herself of his words. She wants to live them every day, never letting him leave her ears.

It hadn't crossed her mind that anything else could come from life. Her first three years was a little recollection: dim pictures of a small fat man catching her under the arms, swinging her, throwing her into the air. She remembers her screams, delighted screams, his eyes, the sound of his voice.

In reality there was probably only one such incident but this memory of her father extends to many repeat plays. He must have lost his concentration. She fell, had a number of stitches to her head. The scar, if she cared to know, was probably still there, but her hair is a mess of black waves now, beginning to hint of grey.

She laughs. 'They say beaches are romantic. But this isn't romance, it's higher, as high as life cut us out to be.' She kisses him and he says, 'High as a storm in winter.'

She has boxed her life from seven to here in nine-year sequences; starting with her dead dad and school as offspring of a lone mother. But jibes against her hadn't been as bad as they had about another girl in the class. That girl hadn't a dad, and never had one. At least her own was dead. And he *was* dead; she figured that for sure at nine because even if her mother were telling her a fib to protect her, the other kids would have known. Their parents would have known all about it. And their kids would have told other kids and then unkinder ones would have spit it back.

She remembers a First Holy Communion day also, or maybe just imagines remembering it. The photograph hung on her mother's and her maternal grandmother's mantel-pieces for all the time she had them in her life. She was told it hung on her paternal grandmother's mantel too, although she never knew that grandmother.

His mouth on hers now is pressing all these thoughts, sweating them almost. She wonders if thoughts articulate themselves with the tongue just as words do. And they are important thoughts, ones she wants to keep. He tells her she has the mark of not knowing a father, but can't explain how he figures that out. She holds him at arm's length and tries to fit a father to his face; but can't, so she just asks to know of his father, that he must have been a wonderful man.

Her love is of the tide; a whisper of sounds that only her outer ears hear as words. Maybe she will no longer need to savour his words, only his sounds. He speaks in snatches; of beauty, landscape, poetry almost, knows what her house looks like even though he has not yet been there. He feels her unhappiness in her place of work too, although she hasn't yet told him of its horrors and boredom.

In her office job she had briefly loved another. That hadn't shown her to be susceptible to falling for other men. An office colleague who was considered knowledgeable of these things would have said she was prone to 'rushes'. That is if it had been known in the office, but it wasn't.

All this, she knows, is unfair to her family, her place of work, her concentration. But she feels no guilt, knows she won't feel guilt. When they get old enough, her sons will want a happy mother. This man will carry nothing but her. Nobody has ever done that before.

To lighten up he guises a great, soft mouse that nibbles her ears, likes her likes, sees her in a sheen that is warm. Suddenly she feels she must try to stop all this, warns him that beyond the rocks is the precipice that we could 'never manage life again without each other'.

The second nine-year cycle was living with her grandmother, in the city, and her first boyfriend. She kept her faith as other girls scoffed; was considered 'a square', not wanting to be in on 'the action'. She often wondered since what 'the action' was. She had reason to believe it meant sex, but still can't believe that then, almost 'light years' before contraception, any of the girls, even the boys for that matter, would have chanced it. She had to wait well into her third nine-year cycle before discovering sex for herself.

Meanwhile she'd studied, loved The Beatles, believes she remembers their 'heyday', even though she was only born in 1963. There is a horror memory too, her least favourite uncle murdering 'Let It Be' at her grandmother's house one Christmas when she was about eleven. Then again she may have dreamt this.

Her man leads her to her rocks now, rocks she knows, was terrified of as a child. But he holds her tight, won't allow her to slip. Consciousness almost leaves her body, this new non-fear near frightening her. There is a pool she knows, jellyfish, jagged rocks, deceptive rocks; these all things she has feared. Her words are still almost whispers. She worries if every syllable reaches his ears or does he miss bits? Will he retain her words as she hopes to with his? He touches her shoulder, releases more words, louder this time. She dispels any fear of anyone prying in this darkness.

He points to rushes. She fingers his hair again and again. His hair is soft wild locks, locks that most men his age would have snipped away. She feels all the other women he has brought here – or some other beach place – disappear from his eyes. He doesn't hide them, but speaks of them, the women he knew.

Still she can't speak of her husband. A husband who married her nine years ago, was still with her, sleeping next to her, still making his love to her. But if he still loved her then his face would still be soft, his tongue not sharpened. Her husband, a doctor, has given her what her ancestors would have called 'security'.

When she threw a fistful of dirt on her mother's grave, she was thirty-two, her doctor husband by her side and two small ones in solemn black. It made her mother 'dead happy'; she laughed afterwards getting drunk with some friends. It was going to make her happy too, content – she was sure of that. She had been until now.

By that fireplace at that pub he hadn't spoken much at all. A breeze that wasn't emanating from anywhere flowed to her skin. The seeds from which he would later make a bed in her ear began to seed. And she was there, in the space within the space of his heart. He will understand all this. Even so, there should be guilt. Guilt is in her breeding.

She doesn't know why she loves him. He tells her of his family, rich in tradition of low-life, middle-class heaven. A place where you are content with little, never demanding the chore of a feeling for art. He has spoken almost truth when with family, he says, while pursuing a higher level that has kept his sanity. 'I have lost my wife to mediocrity,' he tells her, 'have leapt in bounds across rivers that were too wide for my reach.' She laughs again then, at his 'poetry' and louder when he tells her how he 'hasn't fallen as yet'.

She stops laughing, sees his escape as a lucky person does from the perils that mere unfortunates will stumble to, allowing themselves to be crushed. And to think she hadn't been sure! To think that she wondered if he really cared! This, nature has brought to her. It was the beach that did it. She doesn't know or want to know what the future holds. Now that darkness has fallen, the sign has been given, the sign of a sun-filled tomorrow. Nothing will darken her dawn.

War's Orphan & the Sound of Silence

Natascha Graham

There is a stillness, even now,
a silence
of a night stretched too long over and above a world stretched
too thin,
too black – liquorice
All sorts of silence, the sweetness of it left at a train station
Between hanging baskets of primroses and daisies,
To the belch and hiss of the underground,
where damp, never dandelions, spread
And,
Now, she walks with the silence as the sun rises, brown laced boots in long spring
grass, damp and yellowing the closer she walks, matted, yellow, brown, stringy,
mud that sucks and belches through grey flint teeth at thinning soles,
And she stands,
hat pulled down too far over greying hair and blue eyes shielded against the flat
round white shape of the sun behind the straw brim,
behind the rust-brown and moss-green of the great arcing Ferris Wheel that once,
festooned with flags and lights she kissed a girl with toffee apple lips and yellow
ribbons in her hair

in a rattling wooden Ferris Wheel car that brought them over this rust wheel of a

rainbow to heaven,
if only for a moment
– before the air-raid shelters were built, before the name tags were tied to the
lapels of their coats
Before the trains heaved out of the city, great smoking snakes rickety-
clacking to
fields of goats and sheep, cattle and horses, houses that smelled, not of the damp,
rancid stench of the Thames and the mouths of smoke in London Town
where men tipped their hats and women walked arm in arm,
But of Surrey, where the apple and cherry blossom bloomed and the air smelled of
honeysuckle and the sweet rotting pears from the year before.

She hadn't returned.
Not in fifty years.
Only now, she returns, for reasons she won't say,
before the cars of everyone else, before the breakfast bowls that clink in sinks and
the reeling in of workers to the fat cats' grey belly of London.
London.
Who has lost her stillness, her silence,
Her story.
Now, history is the broken English and the bastardised Cockney rhyming
slang,
Not the quiet after the bombs,

when the scream of nazi planes and the screams of those beneath were all
There was.
And the sound of a plane hitting the ground, the bombs, the thud and muffled
boom, a town, a neighbour, gone, and then – (closer still)
the electric sky, a sky
full of wires that hummed and buzzed and roared,
the crack of brick, and stone
the fall of the church spire that crushed the vicar dead in his everlasting sleep
and then,
She remembers,

touches the old fairground sign that remains,
an old fading stump wrapped about the wooden neck with Ivy and the white of
Snowdrops.

She has, now, *her London*, if only for a single
Moment
quiet, before the curtains open, the wait, the breath held, perhaps the most fragile
of all of the silences.
Most unlike the silence of a room full of people when someone is just about to speak
or the silence after the air raid sirens,

Or the silence when you haven't the answer to a question you have been asked or
the hush of a country road that leads to here,
here,
The outskirts of a city reincarnated and never again the same
Where only the rats give the eye of recognition
But for now, however, there is the silence before dawn, an expectant silence, similar
to, though in no way the same,
as the silence before a storm,
when the birds quieten, and a breath is held,
Waiting, bristling,
Waiting, gasping,
Heart beating,
like that afternoon, mid-March, before the bombs dropped and the daffodils turned
from sunshine to acid yellow against a flat grey sky, and the birds,
still,
waiting,
the air too close to bear, and even a breath is too loud.

She sees all of this, now,
In moments,
Standing here, just outside (for she could never go back in)
The first time at London's very edge since the war

For she grew with the
Surrey Downs
She is not the gouche figure in the splintered mirror glass of an old maze punctured
and shattered by glorious oak trees,
She is

Far-flung from the
Smoke in the lanes from Gypsy caravans
And flat-capped men with brown-nosed mutts
Pickpockets
All very Dickensian
she'd heard someone say on the wireless a day, a week, a month ago
All too old fashioned
She touched the fine splintered paint of the Ferris Wheel carriage
Bombs turned lives to rubble and rubble to dust and now
Chain shops link in the underbellies of what were homes but now are houses
with blank-eyed stares of bricked-up windows
and the flat blank eyes of a city that never sees farther than the end of its nose.

The silence of these memories slots into unfamiliar (yet the same)
surroundings
like a black and white photograph held up, out of place but a part of one, just as she
is, standing here,

She who belongs now not to the isolation of London but the solitude of the South
Downs, to a house between hills where cattle graze in the warn away dips where the
doodlebugs and V2's dropped their bombs.
She stands for a moment, then turns, puts it away,
This memory,
Tucks it away in a pocket, with the leaf of the old oak tree, where
Perhaps,
she glimpses the flutter of the flag-end of a yellow ribbon in the nest of a
robin, and
the autumn leaf crunches in the pocket of this old coat with elbows worn thin,
And,
With arms folded, head bowed
she returns,
Back to the rickety clack of the trains,
New now, blue now,
Away from the forgotten but remembered
to perhaps the most beautiful silence of all,
the moment after the door closes and once again you are home.

Purgatory

Shaun O Ceallaigh

SUSIE TURNED THE SCOOTER INTO ONCOMING TRAFFIC, mounted the footpath, and parked between two wheelie bins in the yard behind the newsagent. She then traipsed the short distance to St Luke's Hospital. Her clothes gummed to her skin like clingfilm as she shuffled towards the main gate – a constant stream of morning traffic swarming by.

A small group huddled together outside the gate – smoke rising above them. Five young women, wearing dressing gowns and pyjamas. She recognised the outfit. The first thing the psych nurses do is take away your clothes and give you prison-pallor pyjamas. She passed them, her focus on the pavement.

Once through, she glanced back at the massive billboard:

ST LUKE'S IS A SMOKE-FREE CAMPUS

Ahead of her lay the Outpatients clinic – the old nurses' quarters. Ignoring the warning signs, she trudged across the grass and in through the glass door.

The perfectly square waiting room – five metres by five metres – like a tomb. In one corner, a tall, glassed-in reception counter. Padded chairs around the walls, all bolted to the floor. Three people waited. She scanned them without gawking. A pale, chubby man, in a black overcoat, arms folded, eyes shut, sitting by the door. Near him, a twitchy skinhead in a tracksuit. And in the far corner, a frail boy rocking back and forth in his seat.

She was late. You checked-in on arrival, but the receptionist hadn't shown yet. After sitting a safe distance from the others, she checked the time on her phone, then closed her eyes and focused on her breathing exercises. No one keeps appointments.

*

By twenty to nine, three more patients sat waiting, and still no sign of the receptionist or the doctors. A woman with a beer-barrel gut sat beside her. Rolls of fat sloshed against her arm. A whiff of sprouts about the woman. No one spoke. Now and then, a cough broke the silence.

She stared ahead, trying to ignore the other patients, her gaze fixed on a print-out tacked to the reception counter – an advertisement for a suicide-bereavement helpline. Have you lost a loved one to suicide? it read in slanting, cartoon letters.

'Hey, gimmie two euro.'

The skinhead in the tracksuit had moved to the free seat beside her. She looked at his scooped-out hand jabbing the air.

'Giv'us two euro, like, for a cup of coffee, and that.'

She looked up at his wide eyes. 'What?'

'Come on, Missus, give us two euro for a cup of tea.'

'What ...? No, fuck off.'

'Come on, Missus, just two euro.'

She turned away. 'I said no. Fuck off.'

He got to his feet. 'Fucking c--t.' He returned to his own seat, glaring across at her.

Finally, the receptionist and two Asian doctors swanned through the glass door, the trio chatting and chuckling. The patients watched the exchange until they parted, the doctors going upstairs and the receptionist entering the waiting room.

'Okay,' she said, rounding the desk. 'Who's first?'

The frail boy leapt from his seat and staggered forward. 'I am, I am.'

'Okay, Darren. And who's next?'

The fat guy in the overcoat opened his eyes and raised a hand.

'I'm after him,' the skinhead said.

'And after you?'

'Me,' Susie said.

The receptionist arranged the patients' files. With the folders in order, she rounded the desk again, entered the hall, and climbed the stairs. The boy – desperate-looking – trailed after her.

When she returned the chubby man stood up. 'I'll be outside,' he said, walking into the hallway. From her seat beside the fat woman, Susie watched the coffin-lid door open and close. She checked her phone: ten-to-ten. A glance caught sight of the skinhead – still snarling. She looked at the floor. The fat woman rumbled, her doughy flesh rippling. Another man arrived and sat in the remaining empty seat next to her.

Feeling surrounded, pinned down, lungs parched, she jumped up and caught the receptionist's attention. 'I'm just going for some air.' The skinhead eyed her as she crossed the room.

*

Outside the clinic, at the top of the steps, Susie closed her eyes and slowed her breathing. She looked around and spotted the chubby guy at the bottom of the wheelchair ramp smoking a cigarette.

'Sorry, could I steal a smoke?'

The man glanced over his shoulder, but remained still long enough for her to suspect that he wasn't bothered. Then he turned and held out a box of Rothmans.

'How long have you been coming to the clinic?' he asked as she lit up.

'A couple of years. You?' She blew smoke from the edge of her mouth.

'Ten years this month.'

'Shit,' she said. 'How do you stick it?'

'Has to be done. If I don't turn up, they'll cut my welfare.'

She leaned over the handrail. 'I fucking hate this place.'

'Not surprised.'

'What's your name?'

'Filly.'

'I'm Susie.' She extended her hand. His grip was strong. 'Nice to meet you.'

Behind them, the door burst open and the boy crashed out, stumbling down the steps, and flopping on the grass. A nurse rushed after him.

'Darren, wait ...'

He jumped to his feet and bolted towards the gate. The nurse climbed back up the steps, shaking her head. As she reached the door, she noticed them.

'There's no smoking on hospital grounds.'

'We know,' Filly said, not looking up.

She shook her head again and went inside. Darren paced up and down the footpath, slapping himself in the face.

'What's his problem?' Susie asked.

'He probably expected help. Guess he didn't get it.'

She looked at Filly, about to speak, when a thump from the road, like a sack of flour dropped from a height, sent a crawling ripple over her skin. The boy was gone. In his place, a stationary lorry. The driver jumped from the cab, hands at his head, shouting and calling out to someone.

'Philip?' Susie looked back to see the receptionist at the door. 'The doctor is waiting.'

He tossed his cigarette into the grass. 'So long, Susie.'

She didn't respond, transfixed by the screaming man. People crowded around: a woman on a phone; a man restraining the panicked driver.

Anyone else would have joined them – stood over the lad – but she dropped the cigarette and hurried inside.

*

In the waiting room, no sign of the skinhead – probably upstairs. Susie sat in Filly's vacated seat.

While she waited, she focused on the carpet, trying to block her surroundings. The boy, Darren, was most likely dead. No one jumps in front of a lorry and survives. She'd seen a person die. Strangely, it didn't seem important.

'Susie Lennon?'

One of the doctors stood outside the waiting room. She got up from her seat and he led the way upstairs towards the consultancy room.

In the bare office, soaked in a dead-paper smell, he held out his hand. 'Hello, Miss Lennon. I am Doctor Anand.' His palm was sweaty.

In three years, she never saw the same doctor twice, not since her first admission.

The doctor opened her file to the last page and began reading. 'And how have you been, Miss Lennon?'

'Eh, not great,' she answered.

'Hmm, yes.'

'I have a lot of negative thoughts, Doctor.'

'Hmm, yes. Have you been hearing any voices?'

'Eh, no. Not really. Not since I was in the hospital.'

He turned a page. 'Have you felt like anyone is controlling your thoughts or planting thoughts in your head?'

'No, Doctor. I've just been feeling very empty. I feel … wrong.'

'Hmm … yes. That's normal. Do you have your prescription card?'

She handed him the green card, and he scribbled on the space provided. 'I don't think there's a need to change your medication. Try and get more exercise. We'll see how you are in three months.'

He handed her the card, and she looked from it to him.

'Goodbye, Miss Lennon,' he said, not looking up from the folder.

*

Back in the waiting room, she stood at the desk while the receptionist wrote down her appointment. All the blue chairs were occupied, and two older women hovered in the hallway. She left without making eye contact. It was just gone eleven.

A squad car on the road was the only evidence of the accident. The lorry was gone. A uniformed garda directed traffic, stopping cars coming one way, allowing the patch of tarmac to be avoided.

Susie walked across the grass and stopped to examine the spot where the boy died. A smear of faded pink and yellow covered with sawdust, a tyre imprint, and a single Nike trainer in the gutter.

Two leathery women stood by the gate, smoking. She stopped. 'Could I rob a cigarette?'

'Get t'fuck,' the pyjama-clad woman said, turning away.

She continued on, walking alongside the black railing, cursing the woman beneath her breath. Up ahead, Filly stepped out of the newsagent. He stopped at the doorway, drinking from a Coke bottle, before lumbering away towards the city centre. She watched him go.

She pulled the prescription card from her jacket pocket. After reading the scrawled list of medications, she glanced over her shoulder at the hospital – at the Outpatient building and the garda standing in the road. No help to be found there. She closed her eyes tight and ripped the card into several pieces, then tossed them to the ground. Filly was in the distance now, and she set off after him. It might be interesting to watch what he got up to. She could come back for her scooter. And if she was free of the hospital and free of her meds, she was once again free to do whatever she wanted.

That Bare Hill

Deborah Moffatt

Up there on that bare hill
you wouldn't dare dream
of a summer day, of grain
ripening in the hot sun,
of the kiss of a soft wind
on the back of your neck,

not now, in sleet and snow,
ewes lambing, winter lingering,
a light burning through the night,
fingers fumbling on accordion keys
to pass the time, *The Primrose Polka*,
to speed the season, *The Family Pride*,

dancing feet in the village hall,
cloven hooves in the mucky straw,
footprints all over that damn hill,
the Devil himself out on the floor
dancing with your wife, his tracks
leading straight back to your door.

Roots

Sarah Meehan

buried
in the bottom drawer of the earth
the invisible weavers conduct their work

I think of them as I walk, sealed in rows
in blackdirt dens
low paid, hardworking, practically minded

weaving delicate slippers for daisies
striped socks for tomatoes
gumboots for grass

caring not to tangle
the thin white strings
in those underrooms of darkness

with no one to turn the lights on
accepting jobs of all sizes
no job being too small

for insecure contractors dyeing thread to order
all natural, organic available
quality assured

                 sometimes
I lift a stem from the earth
and shake it of dirt to examine their work

but in the bright sunlight it withers and shrivels
and my hand
holding the pale bones

of what in the underground workrooms
glowed in the dark
                     throws it away

To Understand the River

Helen Kay

is to fall into the sweep of them. Today
they grumble, a cold, cloudy-tea colour
hoiking trees along, like a parent
pushing the kids to be ready for school.
They are all lather and wrinkles
and not now please and out of my way.
They must deal with a backlog of rain
that their soft banks are not built for,
that was not in their contract.

I translate the river tongue,
hear the mumble beneath the gush.
Time to explain the changes
they never voted for, to reassure
that next week they will be slenderly still
pillowed on white stones, sunning their
translucent skin, and massaged by ducks.
They will listen to my ranting babble
while I, framed by a reflection of myself
will stare beyond the shallow to the deep.

Miss Mary Fox

Maria Isakova Bennett

who taught my father in 1938, and taught me in 1972

For her powdered skin
and soap-scented clothes

for her hats worn in class
for the shush of her stockings

for dahlias picked from her garden
still wet with dew

for their newspaper wrapping
for how she placed them

in a cut-glass vase and asked
for prayers for Special Intentions

for giving life even to brick walls in Walton
for creamy flowers full of innocence

for lives condemned to shadow
for stipple, for thumbprint

Up the Attic Stairs

Giles Newington

UP THE ATTIC STAIRS WE WENT, so she could tell me the story.

I'd nearly walked past the church in the old city, the church where my life companion had long ago, as a child, sung in the choir. But then I'd heard piano music, rapid and dramatic and inviting, and had gone inside to listen, winding along an ancient covered walkway to the church door, the scuff of my leather soles on the stone floor wearing away decades.

Inside, in front of the altar, was a grand piano with its lid open. The woman playing it had blue-dark hair that stood up, aided by a yellow and black bandana. She wore a combat jacket and thick cream-coloured trousers and had a ferocious expression on her face as she attacked the keys with swooping, ravenous fingers.

The climactic passage of the music she was playing rioted through the building, sending flocks of invisible panicky ghost-starlings racing through its airy spaces in search of holes or openings or gargoyle orifices from which to exit roof and spire.

Abruptly, in mid-crescendo, the woman stopped playing. As notes fell dead, her angular, lurching figure ceased to be imposing. She huddled herself into harmless domesticated creases as she shifted on the stool and, still seated, leant towards the buggy which, I now saw, had been all the time behind the piano.

The baby's cries were drowning in their own echoes, small sounds cowering from the big building's instant responses. But all noise quickly ceased as the pianist's hands firmly grasped and held up the red-faced infant, blue and wild-haired also, and smiled and shook its wrapped-up figure above her head. Its arms stuck straight out to the sides like glider wings and its legs kicked with a manic, joyous excitement.

The pianist sat the now-reassured child on her knee and embraced it firmly around the waist with one arm, while using a foot to drag a leather bag towards her. She reached down and pulled out a baby's bottle, which she then began feeding to the infant, who caressed and patted it solicitously, appreciatively, as if everything had been done just right, quite correctly.

I became aware of myself standing way back along the aisle of the church, transfixed, unmoving, quaffing freezing air. I knew that if my psychic twin, my life companion, was here, looking up from the wheelchair, I would be told to stop staring – staring like a dork – and look as if I had some proper purpose in this place of ... place of ... worship ...

All was tranquil as the baby watched its mother, whose face I couldn't see.

I marched over towards the door and, with a lordly flourish, put some money in a collection box. Then I inspected the magnificent but heavy cloak I was now wearing, the elaborate hose, the tights, the uncomfortable floppy boots. A large notice on the pillar next to the collection box advertised a concert that evening by the internationally renowned Korean pianist Su Chen, in aid of the women's refuge, but then, when I looked again, also mentioned the public disembowelling of the traitor and heretic Ned Benson at the nearby crossroads in the late afternoon.

I found that the woman and the baby were standing next to me, both covered by a ragged shawl. Her teeth had gone bad.

'I was told,' she whispered, 'that a man would walk in and that I was to take him home and tell him the story. It's about the demise of your life companion.'

The baby stared at me; mockingly, I suspected. But it disguised its sardonic duplicity effectively, turning back with a questioning look to the pianist who was, presumably, its mother.

'That child,' I said, 'is not of God.'

Then, just as I was reaching to see whether or not I had a sword and scabbard, I was startled by the crash of the piano music's resumption, and looked up to see that the pianist, shawl now discarded and bandana back in place, had picked up her recital exactly where she'd left off. The baby, back in its buggy in front of the piano, had lost interest in its bottle, which had become lodged under its armpit, and was sitting up nodding its head and moving its mouth as if it wanted to comment on or compliment the pianist's robust and beautiful playing.

Now clad in purple and white choral vestments, I laid myself down on one of the pews and sniffed at the church's befuddling mixture of odours as I let the music lead me down corridors of grief and speculation.

Why did death so often want its targets entirely depleted before finally felling them? Why did so many of its victims have to be publicly taunted like bulls – immobilised, moaning, pierced with needles, dribbling blood – before the coup de grace was delivered? Why did it have to toy with my life companion's precious faith, the faith that was essential to her existence, before dismissing her from the world?

If she *had* been dismissed from the world, that is. If I could be entirely sure. Yes, there had been a funeral at the convent. Yes, the nuns had contacted me about it. But I had never been allowed to see her body, and the other sisters were blatant in their disapproval of me, uncharitable, and wouldn't share any information about her. There was a death certificate, so I supposed there couldn't be any doubt that she was gone, but still her disappearance from my life a couple of months earlier was left unexplained.

These questions and anxieties again, as always, led me on to other kinds of musing, asking myself why it was that I had chosen so defiantly as my life companion, at such a young age, a woman destined for the religious life, a woman determined to keep her vow of chastity even as she lived in my flat with me for long spells in a parody of married life. I remembered her long-fingered pale hands stretched out to me as we lay in a field in Oxfordshire, the world entirely silent around us, two oddities, ancient teenagers, displaced creatures delivered to the wrong era ... Her blouse had delicate flowers on it ... We'd kissed once, with great tenderness, on the afternoon of the day before, as she left me to go, experimentally, to the prayer meeting she'd promised to attend ... She'd laughed about her plans, but was troubled, I knew even then – as I was – and vulnerable ... The first time we'd ever spoken to each other, I at one point said 'you seem a lost soul' and she'd started crying immediately and without inhibition ... And now, stretching her hands out to me in that field, as if being pulled away from me, the day after that prayer meeting, she told me she was no longer lost, she was in ecstasy, she had fallen in love with God but at the same time with me – and could I live with that? Could I allow her to follow her vocation?

The pianist Su Chen eventually meandered her way through the sweet dying fall that followed the climax of the concerto she'd been playing so compellingly. She stood up after the final tiny note, stretched her hands and fingers (an action imitated clumsily by the baby in its buggy) and packed up a couple of bits and pieces in a shoulder bag.

She pushed the buggy along the aisle of the stealthily eavesdropping church towards me as I sat, back to myself now and dressed in my grey suit, watching from my pew near the door.

Although they didn't look at me, I felt that both the pianist and the baby were weighing up the timbre of my mood as they walked past. I assumed that I was required to follow them along the covered walkway back to the street.

The strident sun outside startled me. There was an overpowering smell of horse dung, and of sewage generally. Crows and pigeons burped and squawked from the low rooftops. Ecclesiasticals everywhere. Very poor people moving carefully, obediently, as if choreographed, in the shadows at the side of the street. Pushing through them, an excited crowd shoving its way along the cobbles. Bustle. Noise.

I kept up my momentum as the pianist hurriedly pushed the buggy a short distance to a timbered house, where she crouched to go through a low doorway. Leaving the buggy by the bottom step, she carried the baby, tight in her arms, up the steep and narrow staircase, floor after floor, to the very top, to the cramped attic room, the baby all the while looking over the pianist's shoulder at me, its eyes changing colour as we ascended.

The pianist left the attic door open, so I pushed on after them into the dilapidated, creaking habitation where there was a bed and a crib and a chair and a small table.

The pianist laid the baby down gently in the crib.

I sat on the bed. The wallpaper was flowery and peeling. There was a pretty patterned rug beneath my brogues. The roof sloped up and away. My guts were in turmoil, as if they were being cut into slices.

The baby looked at me, blinking only very occasionally.

Su Chen sat on the chair beneath the skylight and, engulfed in the sun's brightness, cracked her knuckles loudly and told me the startling story from beginning to end.

The Spoon Lullabies

Janet MacFadyen

Make a mirror of a spoon and catch your image
on its head, mouth stretched open like a fish,
fun-house in the cereal bowl.
Line spoons up like fishing lures, someone
will be in love with them. Maybe I'll
lick sugar crystals from their lips?
Poke spoons in my hair like knitting needles,
like my grandmother? *Come, I will dole you out*
some baby food, some soup, some stew.
A fork and spoon are married on the table, see
them runcible about, spoon with fork's teeth
tuned to sweetness. In deep woods
someone is crooning up a honeymoon,
a crone ladles out the money and the baby
howls *Do I belong here? Where is*
my mummy?
            Behind the carved oval door, a closet.
In the closet, a row of hooks and caught on one
a woman in a mesh of spoons that jangle
as she struggles. Tied to her breast
a cuttlefish. Around her feet a pool
of honey in which the half moon is reflected.
A gasp of recognition. Oh crone,

whose mirror is this? Whose face is this I see?
My dearest heart, my sweetness, first
it was mine, then your mother's, now
it is yours — and baby is next.

Another Coastline

Olivia Kenny McCarthy

Solitary –
I move through the house
reach your room filled with boxes,
your things stacked,
like a heron waiting in the tide.

Outside – a seagull hawks the sky
while I clip back the unruly
brightness of a rose and trowel out
the tangled ghosts of winter.
This is as it should be – solitary

outside, moving happily
through the border, no vertigo,
no cliff of departure, as you roam
another coastline and I trail
my bucket to the compost bin.

Willow

Kurt Luchs

Towering over my childhood
in the backyard was a weeping willow,
and let me tell you
we gave her plenty to cry about,
grinning skulls carved into her flesh
with tenpenny nails, and later
a highwire contraption cutting deep into her trunk
on which we could hang-slide between
the tree and a telephone pole,
a two-way trip to nowhere
always ending with a slam into hardwood
except when we fell off first
and slammed into stony earth instead,
somewhat dangerous but
excellent preparation for life. Other things
the willow witnessed without comment
would have brought the authorities,
if there were any who cared,
to take our parents away in handcuffs
and parcel us out to foster homes.
Yet in this too her silent sobs
were a kind of lesson
and a helpless, useless judgment
on all of us.

The Crannóg Questionnaire

Moya Roddy

How would you introduce yourself as a writer to those who may not know you?

I've been a full-time writer for thirty years. During that time I've published two novels, *The Long Way Home* and *A Wiser Girl*, a collection of short stories, *Other People*, and a collection of poetry, *Out of the Ordinary*. I've written for television including episodes of *Upwardly Mobile* for RTÉ as well as a couple of radio plays. I've also been commissioned to write for stage and film (I love writing dialogue). I've always been involved around issues on women, feminism, social justice, class, and for the last fifteen years or so, spirituality. My work and life hopefully reflects this.

When did you start writing?

I remember having a go at writing a 'play' when I was about eleven mainly because my eldest brother was trying to. I wrote lots of bad stories and poetry for years. It was just something I did – I never thought of it as writing or saw being a writer as a possibility. In my twenties I began taking it seriously (taking myself seriously really), realising someone like me, from my background, could 'become' a writer. Not sure 'become' is the right word.

Do you have a writing routine?

Not as such – I write as much as I can and if I'm working on something or have a deadline I work all day. As it's something I love I never have to force myself – if anything I've had to learn to stop as I probably prefer writing to anything else – especially housework although I'm beginning to appreciate that more – it's very grounding. However, there are periods when I don't write but I see them as an essential part of the process as I feel my mind's working on something or renewing itself. Vital! I think every writer should take up gardening or growing something – that's the best-kept secret!

When you write, do you picture somehow a potential audience or do you just write?

I just write. Sometimes afterwards I think about it but generally I write what I want to write and hope someone wants to read it. No matter who features in my work they are written for everyone.

Some writers describe themselves as planners, while others plunge right in to the writing. Would you consider yourself a planner or a plunger?

A bit of both. I tend to work on things in my head, often in the middle of the night, then at some point go on to the computer and splurge it down. Once I've got a first draft I work and work on it in my head again. I've been blessed with a good memory, which helps.

How important are names to you in your books? Do you choose the names based on liking the way they sound or for the meaning? Do you have any name-choosing resources you recommend?

I tend to 'see' or have a sense of the person I'm writing about before I give them a name. I choose one that suits what they do or how they think and will know somehow if a name is wrong. I've no resources but as I see names as important in real life as well as fiction I notice them and sort of save them up for future use.

Is there a certain type of scene that's harder for you to write than others? Love? Action? Erotic?

I hate putting derogatory or sexist language about women in the mouths of my characters or scenes where women are put down or hurt but it's often necessary for the sake of the story or authenticity. It really goes against the grain.

Tell us a bit about your non-literary work experience, please.
My first proper job was in an office distributing files but I spent most of the time reading as there wasn't a lot of work. Before that I had summer jobs waitressing, in a vegetable shop, working in a home for children. My first job in London was as a filing clerk but I did loads of voluntary work with homeless / single parents / housing organisations which eventually led to a job as a community worker in a law centre. After doing a media studies degree I got a job with a Channel 4 company, first as a researcher on documentaries and current affairs, and later as a writer.

What do you like to read in your free time?
Everything – fiction, poetry, plays, books about environmental issues, women's issues, history, spirituality. I often re-read books several times. My partner and I both read and discuss books voraciously.

What one book do you wish you had written?
The first book I remember wishing I'd written was *Nights at the Circus* by Angela Carter. Then all of Iris Murdoch's work. Last week it was ... I could go on forever.

Do you see writing short stories as practice for writing novels?
They're two different things really. But any kind of writing and the discipline it involves helps with other types of writing. Someone once said short stories are breakfast, dinner or tea whereas novels have to have all the in-between bits and probably supper as well.

Do you think writers have a social role to play in society or is their role solely artistic?
I never write to 'say' something but I always intend my writing to say something. It's how I think. I couldn't write a story just because it was a good *story* (well, maybe I could if it was really good!). It has to have some underlying meaning or transformative element but I don't plan it. It's just a reflection of how I look at the world and my role in it. I think writers have a responsibility to be aware of what they write and the effect

it might have. By definition I think if something's genuinely 'artistic' it's saying something – it's inherent in it.

Tell us something about your latest publication, please.

A Wiser Girl was published by Wordsonthestreet in December last year. It's about a young working-class woman who goes to Italy to au pair but who's determined to turn herself into an artist. On her journey to becoming a painter she finds herself up against the great paradoxes of life – body versus soul, art versus action, sex versus love, happiness versus authenticity and of course obstacles like gender and class. In her review in *The Irish Times* Ruth McKee described *A Wiser Girl* as '... life-affirming ... a novel whose easy tone belies its serious exploration of the authenticity of self, and artistic practice. In these chilly times, it's a blast of Italian sunshine, a sparkling glass of wine.' Enjoy the wine!

Can writing be taught?

Certain things can be taught, craft mainly but I think writing itself or the impulse to write comes from deep inside. What the writer has to do – physically and mentally – is create an environment where it's possible to tap into this – open yourself to it. It also helps to get to know yourself as fully as you can and then as honestly as possible allow that to inform your writing. Then write, write, write – aware you may have to discard a lot of it. I feel it's important to have a vision and an analysis and understanding of how the world ticks or how you tick; then how and what you choose to write is where the 'art' comes in. Since we can only write what we know about this needs feeding and nourishing so reading is a huge part of writing as we learn by osmosis. That and day-dreaming of course ... and curiosity ... it's a lie about killing the cat!

Have you given or attended creative writing workshops and if you have, share your experiences a bit, please.

I've done both. I went to several writing classes/workshops when I started writing and it was great meeting other would-be writers, listening and learning (the power of editing!), reading my work out loud and getting feedback. But for me anyway there came a time when I knew I had to risk leaving the nest and trying out my own wings. Writing groups are a different thing: they can go on for years and be inspiring and supportive – writing is often a very lonely business.

I've also given writing workshops. I taught one at NUIG for several years called *From the Head to the Heart* as I think understanding and sympathising with your characters are key components of writing. In *The Brothers Karamazov* which I've just finished reading you feel Dostoevsky totally understands – identifies even – with the anguish and suffering of the people he's writing about. Another thing I always try to get across is that writing isn't a mystery, it's mainly hard work. You have to sit down and do it and then re-do, and re-do it. As the poster says: Inspiration is 90% plonking yourself in front of the computer or blank page and seeing what happens.

Flash fiction: how driven is the popularity of this form by social media like Twitter and its word limits? Do you see Twitter as somehow leading to shorter fiction?

I hardly use social media but it's possible shorter attention spans may lead to shorter fiction or 'easier fiction' which would be a shame. *The Brothers Karamazov* (over 700 pages) as well as being a rollicking story is crammed with treatises on religion, existence of God, free will, responsibility for crime in a secular society, the individual versus society, etc. Someone I'm sure will reduce it to five lines some day!

Finally, what question do you wish that someone would ask about your writing, and how would you answer it?

Q: How can you help a writer and their work? A: Simple! Buy their books, tell other people about them, recommend them to friends and neighbours and post about them on social media. Writers need readers – it's like oxygen.

Artist's Statement

Cover image: *Rust by Me,* by Bill Hicks

Bill Hicks has been working on a series of original ink and watercolours called DRUMlins for more than 35 years. They have evolved from cartoons to paintings and have been displayed in galleries, published in print media and posted on social media.

Bill says he likes to draw, paint and arrange in such a way that illustrates the relationships we have with the things we use and discard. His characters – the steel drums – he says emphasise that somehow the mundane is relevant, the simple wise and the rusty always beautiful.

He has also created installations, worked in set and prop design, made sculptures and produced several other series of paintings.

He has worked for the Province of New Brunswick in Heritage and Culture and, until recently, was the CEO of the New Brunswick Museum in Canada.

The cover image for *Crannóg* 55 is called *Rust By Me*, part of a body of work for DRUMlins based on well-known songs. This particular artwork is inspired by the song 'Stand By Me'.

No, I won't be afraid as long as …

http://www.brokenshovelbar.com

Biographical Details

Hussain Ahmed is a Nigerian poet and environmentalist. His poems are featured or forthcoming in *POETRY, Kenyon Review, Transition Magazine* and elsewhere. He is currently an MFA candidate in poetry at the University of Mississippi.

Amanda Bell's publications include *Undercurrents* (Alba, 2016), *The Lost Library Book* (Onslaught, 2017), *First the Feathers* (Doire Press, 2017), *the loneliness of the sasquatch: from the Irish by Gabriel Rosenstock* (Alba, 2019). She is a recipient of an Arts Council Literature Bursary 2020. Her new collection, *Riptide*, is forthcoming from Doire Press.

Byron Beynon coordinated Wales' contribution to the anthology *Fifty Strong* (Heinemann). His poems and essays have featured in several publications including *The Independent, Agenda, Wasafiri, Cyphers, The London Magazine, Planet* and the human rights anthology *In Protest* (University of London and Keats House Poets). He is the author of 11 collections of poetry including *The Echoing Coastline* (Agenda Editions).

Laurie Bolger is a London based poet and playwright. Her work has featured at Glastonbury Festival, the Royal Albert Hall, TATE, Sky Arts and BBC platforms. She has been running creative workshops for the past decade allowing people to celebrate their own unique voices. She has written for major brands, charities and visual artists. Her recent work includes *Box Rooms* and *Talking to Strangers*, an immersive performance with a focus on community and kindness, something which features at the heart of her work. @lauriebolger http://www.lauriebolger.com

Niall Bradley is a writer living in Cork. The first page of his draft novel was selected to be read at the Cork World Book Fest 2018.

Jane Burn is a Pushcart and Forward Prize nominated, award-winning, workingclass, bi, neurodivergent poet. Her poems are published in many magazines and anthologies and her next collection, *Be Feared*, will be published in November by Nine Arches Press.

Liz Byrne won the prize for Best Landscape Poem in the Gingko Competition, 2020. She was shortlisted for the Bridport Poetry Prize, 2019 and was highly commended in the Artlyst: Art to Poetry Competition, 2020. Her poetry appears in *The Curlew, Obsessed with Pipework, Orbis, Agenda,* and *Butcher's Dog.*

Helen Daugherty is a copywriter and creative, working for a community library and a filmmaking group in north London. Instagram @helenrdaugherty

Bryce Emley is the author of the prose chapbooks *A Brief Family History of Drowning* (winner of the 2018 Sonder Press Chapbook Prize) and *Smoke and Glass* (Folded Word, 2018), a *Narrative* 30 Below 30 poet and a recipient of awards and residencies from the Edward F. Albee Foundation, the Glen Workshop, the Wesleyan Summer Writers Conference, and the Pablo Neruda Prize. She works in marketing for the University of New Mexico Press and is co-editor of *Raleigh Review*.

Jessamyn Fairfield is a writer based in Galway, whose work has previously appeared in *The Toast*, *Silicon Republic*, and *Viewpoint*.

Billy Fenton lives in south Kilkenny. His work has been published in *The Irish Times, Poetry Ireland Review, Crannóg, Honest Ulsterman, Abridged*, and others. He was shortlisted for a Hennessy Award in 2018, the Fish poetry prize in 2021, and was chosen as a mentee for the Words Ireland National Mentoring Programme in 2019.

Rebecca Gethin has published six poetry publications. She's been a Hawthornden Fellow and a Poetry School tutor. *Vanishing* was published by Palewell Press in 2020 and a chapbook, *Fathom*, was published by Marble in 2021. http://www.rebeccagethin.wordpress.com

Stephen Glennon graduated with an MA in Writing from NUI Galway in 2019. His work has appeared in *Vox Galvia, Ropes Literary Journal* and *The Galway Review* and he is also the author of the book *To Win Just Once*. Born in Dublin, he grew up in the west of Ireland, where he now works as a journalist.

Natascha Graham is a writer of stage, screen, fiction and poetry. Her short films have been selected by Pinewood Studios & Lift-Off Sessions, Cannes Film Festival, Raindance Film Festival and the Edinburgh Fringe Festival. Her plays and other stage work have been performed at The Mercury Theatre, Colchester, Thornhill Theatre, London and Fifth Avenue Theatre, New York where her monologue, *Confessions: The Hours* won the award for Best Monologue. Her poetry, fiction and non-fiction essays have been previously published in *Acumen, Rattle, Litro, Every Day Fiction, The Sheepshead Review, Yahoo News* and *The Mighty* among others, as well as being aired on BBC Radio and various podcasts. She also writes the continuing BBC radio drama, *Everland*, and has an upcoming theatre show at The Lion & Unicorn Theatre, London.

Maria Isakova Bennett works for charities and creates a hand-stitched poetry journal, *Coast to Coast to Coast*. She was awarded The Peggy Poole Award in March 2021, received a Northern Writers' Award in 2017/18, and was poet and artist-in-residence at Poetry-in-Aldeburgh for 2018. She has created collaborative work with over 100 poets from the UK, Ireland, and France. During 2019, she worked with poet John Glenday to create *mira*, a journal and accompanying exhibition. Her pamphlets are: *Caveat* (2015), *All of the Spaces* (2018), *... an ache in each welcoming kiss* (2019).

Helen Kay's poems have appeared in various magazines including *The Rialto* and *Butcher's Dog*. In 2021 she was highly commended in the Welsh Poetry Awards. She curates a project to support dyslexic poets: dyslexiapoetry.co.uk. Her second pamphlet, *This Lexia & Other Languages* (v. press) was published in 2020. She is on twitter at @HelenKay166.

Hugo Kelly has won many prizes for his short fiction and has twice been nominated for a Hennessy New Writing Award. He has been published in several journals and anthologies and his short stories have been broadcast on BBC and RTÉ Radio. He works as a librarian in NUI Galway.

Noel King's poetry collections are published by Salmon: *Prophesying the Past*, (2010), *The Stern Wave* (2013) and *Sons* (2015). He has edited more than fifty books of work by others (Doghouse Books, 2003–13) and was poetry editor of *Revival Literary Journal* (Limerick Writers' Centre) in 2012/13. A short story collection, *The Key Signature & Other Stories* was published by Liberties Press in 2017. He has had short plays produced at Cork Arts Theatre, and the Kenmare One-Act Festival.

Kurt Luchs has poems published or forthcoming in *Plume Poetry Journal*, *The Bitter Oleander*, and *London Grip*. He won the 2019 *Atlanta Review* International Poetry Contest, and has written humour for the *New Yorker*, the *Onion* and *McSweeney's Internet Tendency*. His books include a humour collection, *It's Funny Until Someone Loses an Eye (Then It's Really Funny)*, and a poetry chapbook, *One of These Things Is Not Like the Other*. His first full-length poetry collection, *Falling in the Direction of Up*, was recently issued by Sagging Meniscus Press. kurtluchs.com

Ray Malone is a writer and artist living in Berlin, in recent years working on a series of projects exploring the lyric potential of minimal forms based on various musical and/or literary models. His work has been published in numerous journals in the US, UK and Ireland.

Olivia Kenny McCarthy's poetry has been published in a variety of literary journals, including *Crannóg* and *The Stony Thursday Book*.

Janet MacFadyen is author of five poetry collections, with a new book forthcoming from Salmon Poetry. Her work appears in *Scientific American*, *Naugatuck River Review*, *CALYX*, *Crannóg*, *Sweet*, *The Blue Nib*, *Tiny Seed Journal*, *Q/A Poetry*, and *Terrain*, and is forthcoming from *Osiris*.

Deirdre McGarry is the founder and co-editor of Wexford Women Writing Undercover. She is currently working on a Poetry/Art collaboration to be published by Red Books Press under the title *Light Alchemy*. She has co-edited *Rainbow Jesus* and *The People's Psalms*, and *Small Candles*, an anthology for Amnesty International in Britain.

Liz McManus's second novel *A Shadow in The Yard* has just been published by Ward River Press.

Sarah Meehan's work has appeared in *Cordite Poetry Review*.

Deborah Moffatt's two new collections of poetry are *Eating Thistles* (Smokestack Books, 2019) and *Dàin nan Dùil* (Clàr, 2019). She has won prizes for her poetry in both languages, and her poems have been included in several anthologies, among them *Staying Human* (Bloodaxe, 2020), *100 Favourite Gaelic Poems* (Luath, 2020), and *The SHOp Anthology* (Liffey Press, 2020).

Mary Mullen earned a master's in Writing from National University of Ireland, Galway in 2006. Her debut poetry collection, *Zephyr*, was published by Salmon Poetry in 2010. Her second collection is forthcoming from Hardscratch Press.

Giles Newington worked for nearly 20 years as a journalist at *The Irish Times* and has had work published in *Abridged*, *Crannóg*, *Dublin Review of Books* and *The Honest Ulsterman*. This year he was one of the winners in the Irish Writers' Centre Novel Fair and also won a prize in the Fish Short Story Competition.

Jean O'Brien has published five poetry collections with a sixth, *Stars Burn Regardless* due in late 2021 from Salmon Poetry. She is an award-winning poet having won the Arvon International Poetry Competition, The Fish International Poetry Competition and others.

Shaun O Ceallaigh is a freelance writer.

Feargal Ó Dubhghaill writes poetry and fiction in Irish and in English. He has in the past been shortlisted for a Hennessy Award, was first runner-up in the RTÉ Guide/Penguin Ireland Short Story Competition and was longlisted for the Over the Edge New Writer of the Year Award. His short novel in Irish, *Cathair an Tíogair*, was published in 2015.

Cheryl Pearson is the author of two poetry collections, *Oysterlight* (Pindrop Press, 2017) and *Menagerie* (The Emma Press, 2020). Her poems have appeared or are forthcoming in publications including *Magma*, *Mslexia*, *New Welsh Review*, and *The Moth*, and she has twice been nominated for a Pushcart Prize. Her short fiction has been published in *TSS*, *Longleaf Review*, and *Confingo* among others, and she was shortlisted for the Costa Short Story Award in 2017.

Estelle Price has an MA in Creative Writing from the University of Manchester. She is the winner of the 2018 Book of Kells Writing Competition and her poetry has been placed or listed in the National Poetry Competition (2019), Bridport Prize (2019), Saolta Arts, Bray, Mairtín Crawford Award, Canterbury Poet of the Year, Much Wenlock, the London Magazine, Yorkmix, Manchester Cathedral and other poetry competitions. Poems have also appeared in *Poetry Wales*, *the Paper Swans Pocket Book of Weddings Anthology*, *Three Drops from a Cauldron* and *The Stony Thursday Book* anthologies, the Smith Doorstop *The Result is What you See Today Anthology*, *Mancunian Ways Anthology* and *Deep Time* Volumes 1 and 2.

Maeve Reilly (aka Jeri Reilly) has been recently published in *Utne Reader*, *Dark Mountain* (#19), and has work forthcoming in *The Lonely Crowd* and *Amethyst Review*. @MaeveWriter

Susan Richardson is the author of *Things My Mother Left Behind*, from Potter's Grove Press, and also writes the blog, Stories from the Edge of Blindness. Her poems have appeared in *The California Quarterly*, *Ink Sweat & Tears*, *Rust + Moth*, and *The Opiate Magazine*, among others. http://www.floweringink.com

Colm Scully is a poet and poetry filmmaker from Cork. He has previously won the Cúirt New Writing Prize and been selected for Poetry Ireland Introductions. His collection *What News, Centurions?* was published by New Binary Press in 2014, and you can view his poetry films at https://vimeo.com/user29903251

Marc Swan's fifth collection, *all it would take*, was published in 2020 by tall-lighthouse (UK). Poems forthcoming in *Chiron Review*, *Gargoyle*, *Steam Ticket*, *Coal City Review* among others.

Lisa C. Taylor is the author of two poetry chapbooks and two full-length poetry collections including *The Other Side of Longing* with Irish writer Geraldine Mills (Arlen House, 2011). She also has two short story collections, most recently *Impossibly Small Spaces* (Arlen House, 2018). Her honours include the Hugo House New Works Fiction Award, Pushcart nominations in fiction and poetry, an AWP Spotlight Feature, and numerous shortlist designations, most recently in the Fish Fiction Contest 2020. She is a book reviewer for *Mom Egg Review* (MER) and the fiction editor of *Wordpeace.com*, an online literary magazine. She also runs Whitewater Writing, offering retreats and mentoring. Her books have been taught in colleges and universities in New England. She will have a new collection of poetry published in 2022. www.lisactaylor.com

Laura Treacy Bentley is a poet, novelist, and recent picture book writer from West Virginia. Her work has been published in the United States and in Ireland. lauratreacybentley.com

Steve Wade's short story collection, *In Fields of Butterfly Flames*, was published in October 2020 by Bridge House Publishing. His fiction has been published and anthologised in over fifty print publications. His short stories have been placed and shortlisted in numerous writing competitions, including the Francis MacManus Awards and Hennessy New Irish Writing. He was the winner of the Short Story category in the Write By the Sea Writing Competition in 2019 and first prize winner of the Dun Laoghaire/Rathdown Writing Competition 2020. www.stephenwade.ie

Mark Ward is the author of the chapbooks *Circumference* (Finishing Line Press, 2018) and *Carcass* (Seven Kitchens Press, 2020) and a full-length collection, *Nightlight* (Salmon Poetry, 2022). He was the Poet Laureate for *Glitterwolf* and his poems have been featured in *The Irish Times*, *Poetry Ireland Review*, *Banshee*, *Boyne Berries*, *Skylight47*, *The Honest Ulsterman*, *Assaracus*, *Tincture*, *Cordite*, *Softblow* and many more, as well as anthologies, the most recent of which is *Hit*

Points: An Anthology of Video Game Poetry, forthcoming in 2021. He was Highly Commended in the 2019 Patrick Kavanagh Poetry Award and in 2020 he was shortlisted for the Cúirt New Writing Prize and selected for Poetry Ireland's Introductions series. He has recorded poems for RTÉ Radio 1's *Arena* and *The Poetry Programme*, Lyric FM's *Poetry File* and the podcast *Words Lightly Spoken*. He is the founding editor of *Impossible Archetype*, an international journal of LGBTQ+ poetry, now in its fourth year.

Leonore Wilson is a former professor of English and creative writing from northern California. Her work has been published in such places as *Quarterly West*, *Iowa Review*, *Prairie Schooner*, *English Journal*, etc. She has won fellowships and grants for her writing.

Stay in touch with
Crannóg
@
www.crannogmagazine.com